The Gringo Amigo

The Gringo Amigo

Gary McCarthy

A DOUBLE D WESTERN

DOUBLEDAY

New York London Toronto Sydney Auckland

A Double D Western
PUBLISHED BY DOUBLEDAY
a division of Bantam Doubleday Dell Publishing Group, Inc.
666 Fifth Avenue, New York, New York 10103

A Double D Western, Doubleday,
and the portrayal of the letters DD
are trademarks of Doubleday, a division of
Bantam Doubleday Dell Publishing Group, Inc.

Library of Congress Cataloging-in-Publication Data

McCarthy, Gary.
The gringo amigo / Gary McCarthy. —1st ed.
    p.   cm.—(A Double D western)
1. Murieta, Joaquín, d. 1853—Fiction. 2. California—
History—1846–1850—Fiction. I. Title.
PS3563.C3373G7   1991
813'.54—dc20   91-6921
CIP

ISBN 0-385-41445-5
Copyright © 1991 by Gary McCarthy
All Rights Reserved
Printed in the United States of America
September 1991
First Edition

10 9 8 7 6 5 4 3 2 1

For Mary Melody

The Gringo Amigo

Preface

April 21, 1906
San Francisco, California

In the sunset of my long, fortunate life, I wish at last to unburden myself of a secret which I have carried for more than half a century. A secret that has weighed ever more heavily upon me and which concerns the legend of Joaquín Murieta and "The Gringo Amigo."

I do this fully aware that this secret may no longer be of any significance, historical or otherwise, considering that San Francisco now lies before me a destroyed and smoking ruin. But with the destruction of this great city comes an end to the Joaquín Murieta legend because, somewhere beneath the rubble of this Pacific Museum of Anatomy and Science, with its grotesque anatomical oddities, lies buried the faked head of Joaquín. Buried after being pickled in a jar of alcohol for more than fifty-three years. So too is lost the pickled hand of Three-fingered Jack along with the other horrible museum specimens that attracted thousands of morbid spectators.

You may ask me, why do you now profess to tell the true story of Joaquín Murieta and the Gringo Amigo after so many years of lies? Why sully your esteemed reputation as a California statesman with a matter that is better discarded to the dusty drawers of Forty-Niner history?

My answer—other than the fact that I wish to die with a clear conscience—is that I am forced to tell this tale because I can think of no other way to present to the world the remarkable observations of my dearest friend, Michael W. Callahan, "The Gringo Amigo."

I realize that there are those who will, even after Michael's extraordinary letters and diaries have been published, claim that his account of Joaquín's life is a fraud. They will loudly proclaim that Joaquín Murieta really did die that scorching July 25, 1853, at Cantua Creek under the guns of the California Rangers. But I have faith that more curious and inquiring minds will weigh the accuracy of this literary effort and judge for themselves the true fate of Joaquín Murieta and his "The Gringo Amigo."

This story unburdens me and now that it is finished, I will write no more. What time and energy that remains, I will devote to the rebuilding of San Francisco because, while men die, legends and great cities live forever. Besides, this story is not really mine—its heart and soul spring from the pages of Michael Callahan's letters and diaries, whose entire collection I hereby bequeath to the Historical Society of California.

Senator PATRICK D. RYAN

One

MICHAEL CALLAHAN stood atop the eastern hills overlooking the bay of San Francisco, his long, brown hair held back from his eyes by a battered derby and his feet solidly planted on the good, green earth. He was a tall, angular young Irishman who had celebrated his twentieth birthday in the stinking hold of the *Orion* which had floundered and almost gone down in the heavy seas off Cape Horn. At the height of the howling fury Callahan had gripped the sides of his berth, calmly wondering if his beloved Tessa Glynn would die of a broken heart upon hearing of his death, or simply join the convent and pray for his soul until the Lord called her to His side.

Beside him, Paddy Ryan had prayed even more fervently. Amid sounds of retching men and women, whimpering children and the shrieking wind, Paddy had clutched his rosary beads and begged the Christ for his life and that of the others aboard the ship—especially the little children and their dear, suffering mothers.

The storm had passed, and exactly six months to the day that they had sailed out of New York Harbor, the *Orion* had wallowed into San Francisco.

"Look at them down there," Michael said, pointing to the hundreds of ships that had been driven onto the beaches. "Did you ever see such a sight!"

Paddy shook his head. He was shorter than Michael, with red hair, big splashy freckles and a choirboy's innocent smile. "They just abandon those ships in the mud or in the bay. Leave them to rot."

"And the more's the pity with all those poor devils stranded at Panama City. A man could make a fortune sailing back down there and charging a hundred dollars a passenger."

Paddy shook his head. "It would be blood money and dead wrong to take advantage of them that's stuck in Panama with no passage."

Michael supposed Paddy was right. From the deck of the *Orion,* he remembered the desperate Americans standing on the pier at Panama City, pleading to be rescued from that tropical, pestilent hell. The wrong of it was that they had been the ones willing to pay an extra two hundred dollars to make the Panama crossing in the hope of arriving in California months earlier than those who journeyed by wagon train or sailed around Cape Horn. The scene he'd witnessed from the deck of the *Orion* had been so heartbreaking that Michael still could not shake the image of women and children on their knees, hands raised in supplication as they had begged for deliverance from Panama City. It had turned his heart to stone to hear the captain give the order to hoist sail on his already overburdened vessel for California, leaving those poor, stranded souls.

"If I could," Paddy said, "I would buy every seaworthy vessel in that harbor and deliver the Americans from Panama."

"We haven't enough money to buy a spare gold pan," Michael said.

"I said *if* I could."

"If we had the money, we should have paid the twenty dollars for a ride up the Sacramento River on the steamer," Michael said. "It will take a day longer to walk. We could make that much difference in one hour at the gold fields."

"But if we found no gold," Paddy argued, "then we'd have no money left for food."

Michael was not ready to concede the argument. "This isn't

Ireland during the potato famine. We would not starve. I would kill game."

"With what? A rock?"

"Then we could catch fish."

But Paddy Ryan shook his head. "You heard the man down there at the wharf say that there are more miners in the Sierra streams than fish."

Michael had heard that story, and more than once. He turned his gaze to the west. "Shall we go?"

They could both see a steady stream of traffic moving out of San Francisco, following a heavily traveled road along the banks of the broad Sacramento to Sutter's Fort beside the American River. "Look at them! And more arriving every hour. They remind me of ants moving toward sugar," Paddy said.

"We will have our share," Michael promised, "and it will be sweet when we sail back into New York Harbor, richer than pharaohs."

"My sailing days are over, Michael. I could not survive Cape Horn a second time. And as for the crossing at Panama, I would rather march through Hades."

"Then how will we go home?"

"If I do return," Paddy said, "I'll walk."

"Ha! And what about the wild Indians who would love to have your red hair on the tip of their lances!"

Paddy raised his square pugnacious chin. He was three years Michael's senior and more than a brother. "They would have a good fight on their hands to get it."

Unbidden, Michael's hand reached up to feel the little oilskin pouch held close to his heart. With the pouch was a locket of dear Tessa's hair which he valued as much as life. "We go back home together as rich men—however soon that journey might be," Michael declared. "And then I will wed Miss Tessa."

Paddy bent and pinched at the rich, brown earth. In Ireland, his family had been farmers. In New York, they were mill workers, grubbing not in good, dark soil, but struggling to make steel and tools in cavernous factories unfit to breathe in, unfit for light or laughter.

"I don't know," he whispered, his eyes full of admiration for the green hills, the clear blue skies, the warm sun on his freckled cheeks, "maybe I would stay in California. I have nothing to return to except a family already too big and too poor. These hills are as green as those of Ireland and they say the sun always shines in California."

Michael did not like the idea of losing his best friend. "But if a man is as rich as Solomon, he can chase the sun, live in the northern and southern hemispheres as suits his favor. He will never know cold or feel the hollow of his belly. That's how it will be for us, Paddy."

"How can you be so sure?"

"Because we rotted on a ship for six months and thirteen thousand nautical miles. We suffered the scurvy, we ate the rotten salt pork and beef, and thirsted for fresh water. An even dozen of us died, three went crazy." Michael's blue eyes were strong. "I remember too the man named Elias who shot the captain's mate dead and then dived into the sea and gave himself to the sharks. We *have* earned the right to be rich, Paddy."

"But it might not happen," Paddy said, because, unlike Michael, he had faith only in the Lord whose will could never be predicted.

"Of course it will!"

"Michael," Paddy said, shouldering his own pack with its gold pan, extra clothes and precious shovel head, "have you already forgotten them?"

"Who?"

"The beggars waiting for us along the waterfront. *Hundreds* of them. And there were more on the streets."

"And just what have they to do with us!" Michael demanded.

"Maybe nothing," Paddy said quietly, "but maybe everything. Don't you think that they might already have been to the gold fields themselves? And so, if there is so much gold to be found, why are so many begging?"

Michael's eyes tightened at the corners and he turned to lead the way west. "What they were or are means nothing. The beggars we saw would starve in a henhouse. Sympathy is wasted on them."

"Oh?" Paddy called, hurrying after his taller friend and unable to match his long, angry strides. "Then is that why you gave that poor woman and her brood of hungry children on Market Street *five dollars?*"

"You talk too damn much, Paddy. Save your wind to climb these hills. We still have a long way to go but we are men to be reckoned with."

Paddy had to smile at that, but soon he was gasping for air because he was badly out of shape after the long ocean voyage. His barrel chest was heaving with exertion and he could hear Michael breathing hard too. But they were young and their bodies would soon harden. Unlike his confident friend, Paddy did not expect instant riches. Life had never been easy for the Irish but, God willing, that would change after they struck pay dirt.

For the next three days, they struggled with blisters, sore muscles and biting mosquitos as they joined the flow of Argonauts moving steadily to and from the Sierra gold fields. The first morning along the Sacramento River road, Michael had been filled with good cheer, his spirits so exuberant he had hailed the first San Francisco-bound traveler, jokingly calling, "Did you save any gold for the rest of us!"

"If I had found pay dirt," the thin, limping prospector with red eyes and ragged clothes snapped, "I'd sure as hell not be *walking* back to the bay, gawdammit!"

Michael's wide smile dissolved. He seemed to really see the pathetic man now. "Well . . . well, what happened?"

The prospector glared at Michael, Paddy and the other line of fresh-faced men, eyes fixed upon the hazy outline of the distant Sierras, rosy cheeks flushed with gold fever.

"You all make me sick!" he screamed. "Every damn one thinkin' he's going to 'see the elephant' and strike it rich! Well let me tell you, boys, I can count on the fingers of one hand the number of men who've gotten rich in the gold country. Instead, it's freezing your ass off in rivers and streams so that your bones ache and your back is breakin'. It's bein' so empty in the belly that you don't know if you're shakin' from the cold or from hunger. It's thieves willin' to slit your gullet for your poke and merchants chargin' prices so high that even on good days when you pan an ounce, you can barely keep from starvin'."

The man was so worked up, spittle was foaming at the corners of his mouth, giving him the appearance of a rabid, starving dog. "And it's men fightin' like animals over a claim ten feet square that might not have a speck of gold, and it's Godless mining camps where men work six days a week like brutes so they can get drunk and whore on the Sabbath! Is that what you're all so damned excited about? Is it?"

Michael, Paddy and the others around them were so stunned by the demented fury of the outburst that they were at a loss for words until Michael squared his broad shoulders. "None of us expects it to be easy. Appears to me that Lady Luck didn't shine on you. Maybe if you tried again, then . . ."

The man's cackling laughter sent chills down Paddy's spine. "When I came, I was like you. I had a stake, my health and a boldness in my eye. I never feared I'd not soon be rich. And sometimes I was! One week on Frenchman's Bar I panned a thousand dollars!" he whispered. "Now . . . now I fear only cold and hunger." The man's eyes glinted as he saw the looks of wonder, then doubt. "Sure you don't believe that, looking at me now. But it's true!"

"Then what happened?" Michael dared to ask.

The man threw his eyes off to the west, toward the Sierras and he seemed to struggle trying to remember. "I . . . I don't know," he stammered. "Everything is so goddamn expensive. Storekeepers making all the money now. It just went. That's all. It went."

"Here," Michael said, tearing a half loaf of San Francisco sour-dough bread from his pack. "If you're hungry."

The man's bony fingers were dirty and covered with sores and his nails were broken. But he was quick and he tore the bread from Michael's grasp and stuffed it into his mouth. Muttering incoherently, he shot a final look back at the Sierras then pushed on by as men separated in his path.

"Sweet Jaysus!" Paddy breathed. "I hope we don't see no more like him!"

But they *did* see more. Lots more, though none brought so low or so crazy by their misfortune. Wild optimism was quickly replaced with grim determination. Who could say what might happen in the gold fields? All right, the easy pickings were gone. Now, a man had to be smart, tough, and damned lucky to strike it rich. Well, they *would* be lucky! Strikes were still being made every day. They heard the story about the man who'd found a glory hole the night after a pine tree toppled during a storm. Nuggets the size of duck eggs hanging off the roots! And what about the fella who panned five hundred dollars in five minutes over near Angel's Camp? Why that strike was still paying off a year later and claims no bigger than a blanket were worth fortunes!

Michael heard every success story and repeated it himself over and over, and maybe the others hurrying west did the same.

At night they camped together around fires of driftwood set to burning beside the Sacramento River. They listened to the churning wheels of paddle-wheel steamers carrying men with money along with mountains of supplies to the gold fields. The smart new arrivals listened very carefully to the seasoned prospectors who joined their camp in search of free victuals and a ready audience for their advice and stories.

"You got northern mines and southern mines," a big, humped-back miner with a full beard told his eager audience. "Now the northern mines can be reached by following the Sacramento north most as far as you want. You kin jump off and chase the Feather, the Bear and the Yuba rivers."

"Is that where it's most likely to find placer gold?" a young listener blurted.

The big miner pinned him with his eyes. "Pilgrim, all the easy gold is gone. It ain't like it was in the spring of '49 when a man could pan twenty, maybe thirty dollars a day and sometimes a hundred. Now, it takes luck and hard work."

"But it's still there to find, I mean," the kid persisted. "It must be there or you'd not be returning."

The bearded miner nodded and retrieved a corncob pipe from his vest pocket. "I got a good claim down on the Merced River. I ain't gittin' rich, but I ain't gittin' poor. I got two honest partners and one of us is always gone to San Francisco for fun or supplies. A man working alone, well, he's bound for serious trouble."

"Why?"

"Because he can't leave his claim or it'll be stole! And if he tries to take it back, he'll git shot."

"Well that ain't fair!"

"Fair ain't got nothin' to do with nothin'," the big miner said. "There ain't no law in the camps except that of a rope. It's the strongest and the quickest that win the race. Weak men die or get run off."

The fresh Argonauts grew quiet and somber. They had not heard this kind of talk before and it did not sit well. "So what about the southern mines?" Michael asked. "How's a man get to them?"

The big miner lit his pipe and sucked wetly on it for several moments before he answered. "Pilgrim, all you got to do is follow me and I'll follow the San Joaquin River down to Stockton. That's the jumpin'-off place. From there, it's just a little hike up to the gold country. Just a walk in the country."

"I'll bet," Michael said drily. "That's what they said it was between the Pacific and Sacramento but I got feet full of blisters tellin' me otherwise."

The men laughed when Michael pulled off his socks and shoved his blistered bare feet toward the fire to show he was serious.

"They'll get tough," the big man promised, "same as you will.

But I'm sayin' you might not git rich. In fact, you most probably won't."

Michael's own smile died. "I *will* get rich," he argued. "I'll get rich and I'll go back to New York and marry Miss Tessa Glynn. We'll have a big mansion out on Long Island and a team of white horses to pull a shiny new carriage. I'll have a man-servant and my wife will have a maid. We'll still be Irish, but we'll live like English lords. At night my brood of children will surround me by the hearth and we'll read books and I will tell them stories about the great California Gold Rush and how I struck it rich. And later, after they are tucked into bed, I will take my wife's hand and hold it up to the firelight and watch her diamonds sparkle like the stars in the heavens. And that, sir, is how it will be."

For several minutes, no one said a thing and even the big miner was moved by the flight of Michael's fantasy and the winsome purity of his dreams. But then the man chuckled, breaking the spell. "You're no man for washing gravel in a pan," he decided. "You got the heart and dreams of a poet, so you'll fail. You'll come stumbling back down this trail broke, starving and bitter. And you'll curse me for not turning you around and sending you packing for the blue Pacific before you reach Sutter's Fort."

"As big as you are," Michael said quietly, "you could not do that."

Paddy swallowed noisily, and the big man stopped sucking on his pipe and his bull shoulders humped a challenge. But Michael's expression did not change and his steady gaze did not falter until, finally, the big man's eyes dropped to the flames and he lapsed into a brooding silence.

May 10, 1851

My beloved Miss Tessa:
    Today sunrise began with my spirits on wings as we
followed the Sacramento River, broad ribbon of liquid gold

weaving toward land more fabled than the Seven Cities. My blistered feet seemed to float just off the ground, and I swear I could see your beautiful face on the rippling river waters and hear the sweet music of your voice. But with sun rising over the land, the morning became hot, and I met a ragged man whose story and appearance left me shaken and filled with doubts. All day long, I saw his face instead of yours and there were others like him, not so terrible, but sad.

Tonight I listened to a big man from the Merced River Country tell me I am too much the poet to strike it rich. He was wrong. And despite his prediction, I am again filled with quiet hope, but it is a hope tempered with strong determination. I no longer expect that I will strike it rich the first day, or maybe not even the first week or even month. I realize that luck will play heavily in my fortunes. But however much luck may fail, I will make up with hard work and an unfailing devotion to my purpose, which is to return to your side a wealthy man forever blessed in the radiance of your love.

There are so very many of us, dear Tessa. All hurrying to the gold fields with hopes and dreams. But I sense within me a more resolute heart and a purpose that burns so intensely it cannot be denied. I will find gold, but first, I will find a messenger to post this letter. Most likely that will be tomorrow at Sutter's Fort. We have been hearing bad stories about Sutter and warned that he is dangerous and unpredictable. And this a man who was once the lord of all his land and rich beyond even my dreams. I am learning that striking pay dirt is only half the battle—keeping your wealth is the other!

Your devoted fiancé,
MICHAEL W. CALLAHAN, Esq.

Two

"THERE SHE IS!" Michael said when they topped a low rise of ground and looked out at Sacramento, the gateway to both the northern and southern gold fields.

Paddy grinned widely to see a city of more than twenty thousand. It appeared that most residents lived in tents, but you could see plenty of solid plank buildings, too. And along the docks, there were dozens of barges, paddle-wheelers and even some three-masted sailers which had skillfully navigated up the river with cargo from as far away as China.

The bull-shouldered miner named Isaac, who, the night before, eagerly predicted Michael's failure, had chosen to remain with them, maybe to rub salt into the young Irishman's skin. "Look up there on that northern bluff."

Michael followed the man's pointing finger. He was still smarting from Isaac's harsh assessment of his future and he could sense a hostility in the larger man. They both stood well over six feet tall, but the veteran prospector was a good fifty pounds heavier and Michael was not eager to fight.

"I see the bluff and I'll bet that's Sutter's Fort."

"Least you got that much right."

Michael was impressed. The adobe walls of the fort looked to be nearly twenty feet tall and surrounded by fields and orchards.

"Good Lord!" Paddy exclaimed. "It looks like a castle!"

"It was," Isaac said. "And in these parts, Sutter was the king. When I first came here, he owned over twenty thousand head of cattle, sheep, pigs and horses. There was at least a hundred Indians and half that many whites that worked in his fields and orchards and Sutter made the best apricot brandy and grape wine you ever tasted. But it's all gone now."

"Why?" Michael asked. "Didn't his own man discover the gold?"

"Sure he did! And Sutter was even quick-thinking enough to buy the surrounding land and riverbed around Sutter's Mill from the Indians. But his claim didn't hold up in court and when the news of the gold rush got out, overnight San Francisco became a ghost town! People stampeded across this valley. By the time they got here, they were mean and hungry and they went through Sutter's fields and orchards like a swarm of starvin' locust. They stripped Sutter of everything he owned."

"Why didn't he fight them?" Michael asked grimly. "I would have."

Isaac growled with a contemptuous sneer. "With what? All Sutter's workers ran off to find gold. He couldn't hire enough men to pick his orchards or work his fields. What wasn't stole rotted. His cattle were run off and butchered. Vaqueros took his horses and lit out runnin' for Coloma."

"What about the soldiers?" Paddy asked. "Couldn't he even appeal to the new American government for help?"

"Oh," Isaac said, "he appealed all right. Yelled and raised hell in San Francisco and Monterey. Didn't do him a damn bit of good. Soldiers all deserted. Only the fool officers bound by duty stayed and they weren't about to do any fightin' or shedding of blood."

Michael felt his eyes drawn to the fort. If he were not in such a hurry he'd have liked to meet Sutter. "Is he still up there?"

Isaac frowned. "Could be. He keeps to himself now. Stays holed up in his rooms, usually drunk enough to take potshots at anyone that goes inside his fort without permission."

Paddy shook his head. He knew little about John Augustus

Sutter other than he was a Swiss and had once been a friend of the late Spanish government seated in Monterey and later had bought Fort Ross from the departing Russians.

"Let's go," Michael said, tearing his eyes from the fort, "time is wasting and we've gold to pan."

Isaac smirked. " 'Pan,' you say? Hmmm. I seem to recollect pans were used back in '49. Not anymore, though. Only pilgrims suckered into buying them on the wharves of San Francisco use 'em now. I see you and our friend Paddy bought a couple."

Michael bristled and he might even have taken a swing if Paddy hadn't stepped in between them and said, "All right, Isaac, what do they use now instead of a mining pan?"

"They use a long tom or a sluice box."

"Where do you buy one?" Michael demanded.

"You make them yourself, pilgrim."

Michael's fists balled at his sides. "I'm tired of being called pilgrim! My name is Michael Callahan and, from now on, that's what you'll call me."

Isaac's own fists balled.

"I'll call you whatever I damn well want to call you, pilgrim!"

Paddy tried to hold the two big men apart but he was hopelessly outsized and when Isaac cursed and his fist crashed into Michael's eye, Paddy jumped out of harm's way.

Michael was rocked back on his heels by the heavier man's thundering punch. He shook his head to clear his vision and by then Isaac was already wading in, throwing haymakers. Another connected against Michael's jaw, knocking him skidding across the ground on his backside.

"Come on, pilgrim! Get up!"

Michael took a deep breath. He shook the cobwebs from his head and spat into his palms, and when he started to climb to his feet Isaac swung his heavy boot at his head. Michael ducked, grabbed the man's pants-leg and jerked it straight into the sky. Isaac grunted. When he struck the dirt, breath exploded from his mouth.

"Now you get up," Michael said, moving back and dancing some life into his wobbly legs.

Isaac did not need more than one invitation. Roaring to his feet, he charged Michael, who did not try to meet him head on but sidestepped and dug two thundering hooks into the bigger man's ribs before dancing away.

"Goddamn you!" Isaac grunted, bent slightly with his pain. "Stand still and fight!"

Waving his fists, Michael issued his challenge. "Come on, *pilgrim!* I've been learning mining from you, now it's time you had a boxing lesson."

Paddy shook his head and allowed himself a slow grin. Even in the tough New York Irish slums where they'd been raised, Michael Callahan had earned a fearsome reputation with his fists. He was fast and could hit with authority despite weighing under two hundred pounds.

Isaac charged again and Michael's fists blurred to his opponent's face. They all heard the bigger man grunt with pain, and when he staggered, Michael sledged three tremendous uppercuts to the prospector's thick body, each one sounding like he was thumping ripe melons.

Isaac crumpled like a wet paper bag. He grabbed his midsection, and Michael reared back with his fist but then slowly lowered it and, instead of finishing Isaac, turned his back, gathered his things and headed on up the road with Paddy hurrying along behind.

THEY WASTED LITTLE TIME in Sacramento but instead boarded a small steamer to carry them some fifty miles up the lazy San Joaquin. When they arrived at Stockton, the smaller jumping-off town to the southern mines, they headed straight across the warm, steamy valley toward the southern gold fields and a town called Sonora.

"It's called the queen of the southern mines," a talkative prospector told them early one morning beside a huge California oak tree. "Used to be a Mexican town. Now, there's still too many greasers, but there's more of our kind to keep 'em in line."

"What's wrong with Mexicans?" Michael asked.

"Well, Jesus Christ!" the miner spat. "That's sure as hell a dumb question. Don't you know nothin' about how we won California from the Mexicans a few years ago?"

"I heard about it," Michael said peevishly, "but I forgot the particulars."

"Well, we whipped and run 'em off, we did! Took their damned fancy ranchos and give 'em back to the people. We should have made every Mex in California leave and it was a mistake that'll bear watchin'."

Michael and Paddy exchanged glances. They'd seen a few Mexicans so far, all of them driving freight wagons both to and from the diggings. One had even offered Paddy a twist of his black tobacco. They didn't seem like bad folks. And they were God-fearing Roman Catholics, same as the Irish.

The prospector, it seemed, could get worked up on the subject of Mexicans. "Greasers will stick you with their blades when your back is turned. They'll steal your poke and rape your women. Me, I'd as soon put a bullet through them as quick as I would an Indian or a Chinaman."

As soon as they could, Michael and Paddy left the prospector and found their own way along a well-traveled road that lifted off the warm Central Valley floor into the green-forested foothills of the Sierras. Soon the air was cooler, the scent of pines was tonic, and their weary footsteps seemed lighter as they entered a canyon and beheld Sonora on a Sunday with a church bell echoing up and down the canyon, calling those few who had not abandoned their faith for gold.

The bustling mining camp was the kind of settlement that Michael had always pictured as being typical of the wild west. Its wide, dusty street was filled with interesting and boisterous characters. Freight wagons, mostly pulled by mules, vied for supremacy with pedestrians and horsemen. Michael counted dozens of saloons, each supplied by the Bauman Brewery on Washington

Street. On all the narrow side streets, he saw impressive adobe villas with lush hanging plants and flowers blooming in bright profusion.

Sprawled in front of the two-storied Gunn Adobe, four Mexicans gaily strummed guitars and flashed gold teeth whenever one of their compadres dropped a coin into an upturned sombrero to show his appreciation for their music. In fact, Michael noticed that Sonora's population was at least fifty percent Mexican. Many owned stores and Spanish seemed to be as common a tongue as English.

"Look at that," Michael said with a grin as he dug an elbow into Paddy's ribs. "Ain't she a beauty!"

Paddy's eyes followed Michael's to rest on a Mexican señorita wearing a white, low-cut blouse, a red skirt and a pink rose in her glossy black hair. She was probably in her early twenties and smoking a thin cigarillo. Smoke trickled from her nostrils. She gazed up at a handsome vaquero, who sat relaxed and almost knightly upon a magnificent dapple-gray stallion.

The pair were chattering happily in Spanish. The señorita offered the vaquero a smoke from her cigarillo and, to Michael at least, the resulting exchange was almost sensuous as the vaquero took the woman's cigarillo and rolled it between his lips. His mustache bristled a little and his hot, black eyes never left the young woman's pretty face as he smoked and she stroked the neck of his fine horse. As a boy, Michael had read stories of Cortés and the other great conquistadores of Spain. Even without a lance or armor, this man seemed a throwback to those great adventurers. The Mexican had an indefinable air of detached intensity that could never be imitated.

"I don't think anyone is going to run *them* out of Sonora," Paddy said with admiration.

"Who'd even want to?" Michael said.

The vaquero was dressed in his Sunday finest, with black and silver-stitched sombrero to match his fancy shirt and bolero jacket. His pants were skintight over his rider's muscular legs and decorated with silver coins sewn in along the outer seams.

He wore a red silk sash around his throat and a rakish mustache waxed and tipped like daggers. Unlike most miners', the vaquero's ornate pants were not tucked into his boot tops but flared over his boots and stirrups so that only his huge silver-roweled spurs were visible. Michael saw the outline of a knife sewn into his boot top, and on the vaquero's hip rested a beautiful pearl-handled Colt revolver. Coiled against his pommel was a rawhide reata that must have been sixty feet long.

Suddenly aware that they were being stared at, the Mexican couple turned to gaze at Michael and Paddy. Their eyes were unfriendly and even a little challenging. Compared to the Mexicans, Michael felt shabby and colorless. He quickly glanced away, as self-conscious as if he had been eavesdropping on a pair of lovers.

"Adios, Rosita," the Mexican said.

"Adios, Joaquín," the woman replied in a husky voice.

A moment later, the vaquero rode by and Michael caught a glimpse of his profile with its aquiline nose, high cheekbones and prominent jaw. As Joaquín's fine stallion danced down the street, tossing its head and putting on a show for everyone, the vaquero seemed a part of his horse and completely relaxed.

"He must have been born in a saddle," Michael commented.

But Paddy's mind was on his stomach now. "Let's find something to eat!"

It was easy to locate a small cafe, but when they sat down and read a crudely printed little menu, they made a quick exit.

"Did you see those prices!" Paddy exclaimed with astonishment. "Meat and potatoes were five dollars!"

"Coffee or tea fifty cents. Cheapest thing on the menu was soup for a dollar a bowl," Michael said, reaching into his pants and pulling out the last of his money. "I've got exactly eight dollars after paying for the steamer down from Sacramento. What about you?"

"Eleven and some change."

"Maybe we'd better buy meat and flour," Michael said, "and

then tomorrow we'll head up to the diggings and get to work early."

Paddy nodded his head in agreement. He was of shorter than average stature, but he was strong and could eat prodigiously. Besides being seasick most of their voyage from New York, he'd been constantly hungry and Michael knew that food often dominated his mind. When they had boarded the *Orion,* Paddy had weighed a corpulent 190 pounds. Now, he was probably down to 150 and his patience had diminished along with his waistline. He often talked about meals he had enjoyed and hoped to enjoy again. Michael, always lean, tried to show interest in this part of Paddy's conversation, but his heart was not in his belly like it was with Paddy.

"There's a store over there," Michael said. "Let's buy some groceries and get directions to the best diggings."

Groceries, as it turned out, were almost as expensive as eating in the cafe. Grudgingly, they bought two pounds of salt pork at four dollars a pound, salt, nine dollars' worth of flour at three dollars a pound and a bag of dried apples for two dollars.

"We'd better find some gold before this food is gone," Paddy said uneasily, " 'cause we sure aren't going to fill our bellies off our good looks."

"We'll find gold," Michael promised with confidence. "We just need to get going now that we got directions to the best diggings."

"Yeah," Paddy said, "I sure hope that fella inside the grocery wasn't giving us bad advice."

"No reason for him to do that," Michael reasoned. "If enough people like us don't find gold, we can't buy groceries and he goes broke, too."

Paddy nodded because what Michael said made good sense. So they stuffed their precious few groceries into their packs and chewed a hunk of beef jerky hot enough to smoke a Mexican's eyes and then plodded wearily out of Sonora, heading for a place called Bullion Bar about five miles up the road.

"The man said it was a new strike and we might be able to

stake ourselves a decent claim," Paddy said. "You know how to do that?"

"Nope, but it can't be too hard to find out."

IT WAS EVENING by the time they reached Bullion Bar.

"Jumpin' Jaysus!" Paddy whispered. "Look at em!"

Michael swallowed and his heart fell to his blistered feet. The hillsides on both sides of the creekbed were crawling with miners. There wasn't a square foot of Bullion Bar that had not already been claimed and whose rocks and gravel were not being sifted and sorted.

"Well," Paddy said bleakly, "what do we do now?"

"We find another stream and just start working the gravel," Michael said. "I don't know what else in the world we can possibly do."

"Neither do I," Paddy said, "but can't we just make camp right here and go on tomorrow? Maybe things will look a little brighter to the both of us."

But Michael shook his head. "Still an hour of daylight left and we need water. If we tried to drink from the stream here, we'd probably get shot. I say we go on up the stream however far it takes to thin out the crowd."

"All right," Paddy said. "But dammit, we're going to eat us a good dinner and I don't care how late it is!"

"It's a deal," Michael agreed as he began to skirt the feverish mob that was tearing up the streambed at Bullion Bar.

Three

September 17, 1851

My Beloved Miss Tessa:

Just over four months have passed since we arrived in the gold diggings and was sure I would be rich by now. Sad to say, I have never been poorer. Paddy and I are working from dawn to dusk and, although we are earning ten dollars a day, we can barely survive because of the high prices. Coffee is $6.00 a pound, thin woolen blankets $25.00 each, boots are $70.00– $100.00, socks $10.00, pants $30.00 and even candles are $1.00 each! So you can see why a man has to make a big strike to go ahead out here.

We have finally scraped enough money together to buy planking for a sluice box, we have still had no luck. It would be very discouraging if it were not for the fact there are many like us. There is no accounting for luck in these gold fields. Fifty feet downstream, a cry might suddenly be heard, "Eureka," which means a single large or a pocket of small nuggets has been found. This creates a whirlwind of excitement and we labor feverishly for another day or two, each moment expecting to be similarly blessed, but we are always disappointed.

Our dear friend, Paddy, talks of nothing but food. He is driving me crazy but I cannot be angry with him. He does not have our dream to hold him to a purpose. When he is not talking about food, he talks about starting, as you would expect, a grocery store! This gives us something to laugh about even in our darkest, hungriest hours because it is a certainty that Paddy would devour his own profits.

As Paddy is obsessed by food, I am obsessed by the thought of you and of the moment I can return a rich man who will at last marry and give you the life of comfort that you so richly deserve.

I must go now. Daylight is coming and the more I work, the sooner I will be at your side. There is much tension here now. A tax has been passed against those of foreign blood. It is called the Foreign Miner's Tax and is meant to drive the Chinese, Mexicans, Chileans and others off their claims. We expect trouble and I confess that I have little sympathy for the tax myself and would not join others in its enforcement. But this is of no interest to your sweet, pure heart and so I bid you farewell. As soon as I can spare a dollar required to post this letter, I will do so.

Your devoted fiancé,
MICHAEL W. CALLAHAN, Esq.

MICHAEL FOLDED THE LETTER and inserted it into a soiled envelope. He ran his bruised fingertips over the smooth paper and closed his eyes for a moment, visualizing Tessa Glynn's lovely face. Her hair was light brown like his own, but that was where any similarity between them ended.

Tessa Glynn was petite, soft and perfectly rounded in all the right places—he was tall, loosely hung together and jerky in motion. Her smile was quick and impish—his was slow, but wide. She moved in tremendous bursts like a flaming star, often shooting from one thing to the next—he warmed up like an old horse too long in harness, but pulled long and steady once he set to a task. He was patient—she was impatient. She was beautiful —he had the face of a funny clown. She loved dancing and music

—his music was found in poetry and prose. She was romantic—he was quietly and completely crazy with love.

"Paddy," he said, hearing the first prospector's shovel bite metallically into sand and gravel, "we'd best get to work."

Paddy grunted but did not move.

"Paddy, the sun is up."

"I don't care," he moaned. "I don't give a damn."

"Sure you do!" Michael forced a laugh. "Today might just be the day when we finally strike it rich! This is a new camp with a new chance to hit pay dirt."

Paddy stared at Michael's chiseled face. "Where are we today?"

"Whiskey Slide."

Paddy blinked but nothing in his slack expression indicated that the name meant anything. This was confirmed a moment later when he grumbled, "Whiskey Slide? What about the others? In four months we've been through so many gold strike camps that I can't remember all their names."

"It doesn't matter."

Paddy sat up and savagely knuckled his eyes. "Poverty Flat—we nearly starved to death there. And Hungry Camp—dear Lord I'm *always* hungry! Dead Man's Gulch. Gouge Eye. Murderer's Bar. They're all named for hard times. Michael, I'm finished! I can't take the hunger and the disappointment any longer."

"But . . ."

"No!" Paddy lowered his voice. "Look," he said, urgency creeping into his voice, "I *hate* prospecting! This is not working."

"But it could. Four months isn't that long!"

"It has been to me."

"But we made a pledge not to quit until we struck it rich!"

Paddy scoffed. "You still don't see it yet, do you? Michael, the only people getting rich are the ones that are mining our pokes! It's the merchants and the damn farmers out in the valley who charge us a dollar for a worm-ridden apple, fifty cents for a shriveled ear of corn. They're the ones that are prospering."

Michael stood up. "So we're back to starting up a grocery store and you without a pinch of gold to spare."

Paddy hurled his blanket aside and crawled to his bare feet. "I'm going to work for Mr. Potter who just opened up a new store in Hangtown," he proclaimed. "Mr. Potter said I could come to work for him at his store. He said I'd be good at it and maybe I could buy into a partnership in a year or two."

Michael's jaw dropped. "A year or two! My God, man! In a year or two we should be rich and back in New York."

"I'll never go back east again! I've told you that again and again but you won't listen!"

Michael turned away. Two weeks ago they'd celebrated finding a nugget worth seventy-five dollars. They'd bought whiskey, the planking and food. That first night of celebration, they'd finished the whiskey and renewed their pledge to get rich. But since then—no gold, and now Paddy was saying the pledge was gone too.

"I got coffee brewing," Michael said as he moved back toward the fire he had tended since before first light. "You like coffee."

"I don't want any."

Michael whirled around. "You *will* have a cup of coffee! You'll have it with me before you leave for Hangtown."

"All right," Paddy sighed. "All right. A cup of coffee, then."

The boiled coffee was so weak it was the color of a Chinaman's tea. They sat sipping and blowing on it until it was warm and then they both set the dregs down and stood up, neither quite knowing what to say or how to part still friends.

"You could come too," Paddy blurted as he grabbed his pack. "My God, it's not like this claim will be any different than all the others! You'll probably earn nothing here."

"I know."

"Then come with me to Hangtown where a man handy with tools can earn five and ten dollars a day! Those are high wages, Michael!"

He nodded. "Yes, they are. But ten dollars a day won't make a man rich enough to buy a white carriage and white horses so that he can look his fiancée in the eye and tell her that he 'saw the elephant' and bested the big sonofabitch."

The hope went out of Paddy's eyes but he couldn't quite leave it alone. "Michael, you could find a good job and save money. Maybe we could open a store together next spring if we were both earning wages and saving our money."

"No! I promised Tessa the moon and stars and, before I'm done, she shall have them."

Paddy ran his hand nervously across his mouth. He seemed to struggle, then made a decision. "Michael, I've been wanting to tell you a few things about . . . about Miss Glynn."

Michael's eyes narrowed. "Take care what you say, Paddy! By God, watch your tongue, now!"

"But you're killing yourself for her and it's not right! And you expected me to do the same. Michael, Tessa is a beautiful girl. But you aren't the only young man with eyes for her."

Michael's fist shot out and he grabbed Paddy by the shirtfront. "If you got something to say, then spit it out, man!"

"She's got other . . . other *friends* that have come to these gold fields, all promising to come back rich and marry her."

Michael bashed Paddy in the face so hard he slammed up against a pine tree. Shaking his head, he choked, "I don't want to fight you."

Michael took a step forward. His expression was murderous. "I give you no choice! Now put your hands up!"

"No," Paddy said. "Up or down, it would end the same way. If you mean to whip me, then do it."

Michael cocked his fist back. Paddy waited quietly. "If you want to hit me for telling you the truth so you don't kill yourself any longer over that girl, then hit me."

With an anguished sob, Michael Callahan turned away and staggered toward the stream. Paddy watched his friend grab a shovel and furiously toss rocks, sand and gravel into their sluice box.

"I'm sorry," he said, not very loud. Not at all loud enough to be heard over the sound of running water and of Michael's shovel biting into the rocks. "Good-bye."

It was noon before Michael's strength failed and he sank to his knees in the water and laid his forehead against the sluice box. He twisted his head around and stared at his camp. Paddy, of course, was gone.

Michael turned back to the river and his eyes dropped to the riffle bars of his sluice box where the heavier gold would be trapped. Out of habit, his sore fingers probed the soft mass behind each riffle bar, discarding small stones, searching for a nugget or at least some gold dust.

He found neither.

"Dammit!" he raged, coming to his feet, grabbing the sluice and knocking it over on its side. "Goddammit!"

Miners up and down the stream glanced at him but they did not stop working or even pause to stare because men went crazy with frustration and desperation every day of the week in these hills. Nobody much cared. There were already too many men working the rivers, streams and even the dry washes. One less man made no difference.

Michael stared at his sluice and at the stream made muddy by the hundreds of miners whose claims stretched above his own. This claim, like most of the others he and Paddy had worked, had already been picked over, not once, but probably several times.

A smile spread across Michael's face that was sure to give those within sight the idea that he had gone loony. To further reinforce that impression, he sat down in the stream like a hot dog. The water was up to his chest now and, to keep himself from being carried away, he grabbed onto his sluice.

"I been doing it all wrong," he said to himself. "Instead of chasing after every strike and always arriving late, I've got to start my *own* strike. I've got to be the *first* one there instead of one of the last."

That was it, pure and simple. From this moment on, he would

no longer follow the herd. He would head off on his own until he found a strike and made his fortune. No more running with the pack no matter how loud or insistent its clarion call.

That very morning he pulled his stakes and followed the Stanislaus River into the higher country. About noon he heard gunfire, and, since he was not armed, he moved slowly through the trees until he arrived at a point overlooking a wide bend in the river and saw a large Mexican mining camp. It was not the first that he had ever seen, but it was one of the largest, with perhaps twenty men in a tense knot standing on a sandbar beside their long toms and sluice boxes. Off to one side and apart from the confrontation stood a half dozen women and children. All of the men were being held at gunpoint and Michael hunched down behind a rock, unsure of what was going on.

"Each of you greaser bastards either pay the twenty-dollar-a-month head tax, or you pack up and leave this county!" a man on horseback wearing a black suit and a string tie demanded. "It's the law, and by God it's long overdue. Now for the last time, pay up or move on!"

The Mexicans looked afraid and Michael guessed they had every right to be since they were outnumbered by heavily armed men.

One of the Mexicans, a fellow in his thirties wearing sandals and dressed in a faded serape, dared to protest. "But, señor, we do not have that much money! And this is *our* claim."

"It ain't spit if you don't pay the damned tax, señor!"

The Mexican removed his old straw hat and rolled it in his thick brown hands. He turned to several of his peers and they talked in Spanish, arguing low and fast to themselves.

"Goddammit, Les, either make 'em pay the tax, or let's drive the whole damn bunch south!" a rider complained as he impatiently shifted a double-barreled shotgun against his pommel.

"Shut up, Bert! We agreed I'd do the talking. No one is backing down. You Mexicans are leaving now!"

The Mexican who had become the spokesman turned, growing angry, and with a single outburst silenced the others, then turned back to the riders. "Señor," he began, trying but failing to dredge up a smile, "perhaps we could pay a hundred dollars for five of us to stay. The others could—"

"Oh no you don't!" the man in the suit exclaimed. "I can see that little game in a hurry. You either *all* pay, or you *all* go! Women and children too!"

The Mexican's hands throttled his straw hat and his voice trembled, though he struggled to conceal his outrage. "But, señor, this is unjust. It would take many hundreds of dollars for us to stay!"

"Then you'd better get moving."

"But, señor! We have worked hard to—"

Whatever the Mexican was going to say next was lost in the thundering explosion of the shotgun. The Mexican screamed and began to hop around. The man with the shotgun emptied a second load between the Mexican's bare feet, causing him to topple into the river.

Michael's blood went cold. He jumped up and raced out onto the bar yelling at the top of his lungs: "Stop it! Stop it, damn you!"

His sudden appearance caused everyone to swing around and stare at him.

"Who the hell are you?" Bert demanded, reloading his shotgun.

In answer, Michael charged the man and tore the shotgun from his hands. In a murderous rage, he smashed the shotgun's stock to splinters and hurled it into the river.

"You've got no right to shoot or run these people off their claim!" he yelled. "No right whatsoever!"

When Bert saw his shotgun go spinning into the river, he reached for his sidearm, a curse on his lips. His horse was jumping around and that was the only thing that saved Michael's life as Bert began to fire wildly.

Michael felt a bullet crease his cheek. When he slapped at his face it was covered with blood. Men were shouting. Bert, in his frustration, piled off his horse, raised his pistol and would have shot Michael to death if a Mexican hadn't put a bullet through his chest. Bert staggered backward and toppled into the river as the wounded Mexican was dragged up on the bar by one of his companions.

All hell broke loose as Mexicans and white men opened fire. Michael saw a horse with its dead rider's boot caught in a stirrup plunge crazily up the river and disappear into a tangle of growth. Other horses unseated their riders, and Michael saw the Mexicans whirl and chase their women and children into the brush and trees.

The white men were probably not expecting an all-out gun battle, but that's what they got and, since they were on horseback and the Mexicans had the advantage of solid ground, three of the riders died in the first heavy volley. The moment their pistols were emptied, the riders whipped their horses back down the river and the Mexicans sprinted for the cover of the trees.

Only Michael, the three dead horsemen and a dying Mexican, who could not have been out of his teens, remained. The boy was trying to pull himself toward the trees but going nowhere. Michael ran to his side and rolled him over and raised his head. "Hang on!"

The boy's eyes were wide and staring. He fought to whisper something.

"What is it? What are you trying to tell me?" Michael pleaded, leaning forward to hear.

"Run, señor!"

Michael twisted around to see a lone horseman charging back upriver, his galloping horse knocking huge sheets of water into the air at every stride. Michael grabbed the boy's old pistol, but when he raised it and pulled the trigger, the hammer dropped on an empty cylinder.

Two bullets ate the wet sand beside him. Michael froze in panic, knowing he could not escape the charging horseman, but he did not have to because a heavy volley boomed from the trees and the horseman was plucked from his saddle and flipped over backward into the river. The horse raced past Michael, stirrups flapping like broken wings.

"Run, señor! Run!" came a shout from the trees.

Michael ran for his life. He plunged blindly into the thickets and struck a tree, reeled and staggered on deeper into the forest until he at last heard the gunfire and the curses recede into silence.

When Michael could run no more, he collapsed on the ground and lay gasping for breath. A blue jay high above peered down and mocked him. As his heart slowed, Michael knew that he had to return to the Mexican claim. Not only to see if the boy was still alive, but to find his pack, which he had discarded at the edge of the forest. In it were all his worldly possessions, including a few ounces of gold dust.

It took him nearly an hour to move stealthily back to the Mexican camp. When Michael neared it, he crouched down and peered through the brush. Except for his bullet-torn cheek and the slashing hoofmarks in the sand, nothing gave evidence that men had fought and died on this peaceful and nameless sandbar along the Stanislaus River.

Michael shivered. He had never felt so insignificant. He was seized by a powerful urge to be rid of this place of death. Quickly shouldering his pack, he stumbled away from the Mexican bar, striking out for the high country, where he could be alone.

Four

MICHAEL HIKED up the Stanislaus River until there were very few prospectors. Those that he did meet spoke discouragingly about the fact that the diggin's were so poor that a man did not stand a "Chinaman's chance" of finding enough gold to keep him in pork and beans.

"There's been hundreds like you come up in this high country," a dispirited prospector said, "and I been one of 'em. I reckon I figured that I would head out on my own and maybe make a strike. Get a camp named after myself and be somebody for the first time in my life. But it didn't happen."

Michael looked past the man and on up the river canyon. "How long have you been prospecting up here?"

"Sixteen months. Worked right on through last winter, I did. You'll get snow at this elevation. It'll come before too long, that I promise. You'll freeze to death if you don't starve first. Ain't nothin' but a few greasers and Chinamen working up here 'cause they can't afford to pay the tax in the better diggin's downriver."

"That Foreign Miner's Tax," Michael hissed, "that damned bloody tax. It isn't right!"

"Sure it is! We need it to protect us," the miner argued. "The Chinaman, now he don't need much of anything to live on. He can work a claim that's been picked clean and still prosper and save his dust. He'll stay in the California gold fields, three, maybe four years and then he'll go home a rich man."

"So what's so wrong about that?"

The prospector raised his eyebrows. "So what's *right* about it! A damned little Chinaman comes to America, contributes not a damn thing, takes out American gold and then leaves. And all the while, he looked down his little nose at us. Did you know they're so all-fired high-falootin' they consider themselves superior to the white people?"

"No."

"Well, they do! And the Mex ain't much better. Oh, he'll shuffle and act humble enough when he's with his betters, but I seen 'em at them fandango halls, drinkin' and raisin' hell. They hate all us gringos for winnin' California and drivin' 'em off them big ranchos. And them vaqueros are the worst of the lot. They ride around like they was the masters of the land."

"They're superb horsemen," Michael said, remembering the one he had seen in Sonora by the name of Joaquín.

"They're all show and nothin' for work."

Michael had heard this kind of talk until it stuck in his craw. "Guess I'll be hiking up the canyon now," he said, turning on his heel and walking on.

"You'll starve out or freeze!" the prospector called. "Either that or the Mexicans will put their hog stickers in your belly some dark night. Mark my words!"

A week later, Michael chose a permanent camp inside a large rock fissure that split a rock wall fronting the Stanislaus. The fissure ran about six feet wide and a hundred feet deep. At its end, a trickle of water bled down the mossy rock walls to form a pool that seeped into the ground and no doubt fed the river. Pine and aspen crowded the walls of the fissure and there was a low ledge where a man could huddle and use the rock walls to deflect the heat of his campfire. Because the walls of the fissure were shot with quartz, Michael had a hunch that the fissure might yield some gold. Besides, the river was too cold to work anymore. After an hour of working it his hands would be numb and his feet and ankles aching so that he could barely walk. It was time to leave the water and try dry diggings. With the rivers and streams about picked clean, more and more prospectors were working dry claims.

Some months earlier, in the town of Columbia, Michael had handed over two pinches of gold dust to hear a professional geologist lecture about how to locate gold in the dry digging. Unfortunately the geologist had been a blowhard, using big, fancy terms that no one understood. He'd paced back and forth before an increasingly hostile audience of miners who finally began to demand a refund.

"All right!" the geologist had shouted, still more angry than scared. "Maybe I can bring it down to your simple level. Gold is unlike most metallic elements because it occurs in a pure state. And millennia ago when the earth was a molten mass boiling and bubbling like scorched porridge, the melted gold became chemically bonded to other minerals—especially quartz. When the world cooled and its surface buckled to form the mountains, veins of quartz were exposed. Eventually the veins of quartz eroded, exposing the bonded gold, which was washed down mountainsides by rain and melting snow. The heavier gold ended up in the rivers but the *source* still remains in the high mountains bound in the veins of quartz."

This had been a revelation to Michael. He had jumped to his feet as if he'd sat on a nail! "Shut up, all of you!" he'd bellowed. "What the man is saying right now is the heart of the secret on how to find gold!"

But the audience had had enough. They were on their feet stomping and threatening to tear the room apart if not given a refund, which was quickly promised. The geologist had stomped off the stage amid hoots and catcalls of derision. Michael, however, had wanted to hear more and rushed outside to catch the lecturer as he was hurrying away.

"Leave me alone! Get your damned refund like the others!"

"I just want to know one thing. Were you trying to tell us that if we find quartz we will find gold?"

The geologist had not slowed his rapid step. "My friend, I'm saying that the chances of finding gold in veins of quartz are far better than finding gold in any other type of rock."

"Well, dammit," Michael had cried, "why didn't you just say that in there!"

"Because no one would pay two pinches of gold to hear it explained in such simple terms."

"I would have."

"Then," the geologist had growled, "release your hold on my arm and I hope you profit greatly from my education."

"I will," Michael had vowed.

From that day to this, Michael had looked for deposits of quartz. He'd found some, but no gold. Still, he believed the geologist, and never before had he seen so much quartz as this. Why, the upper walls of the fissure glistened and Michael was sure his luck was finally about to change. All that first day that he spent in the rock fissure, Michael admired how the shafts of sunlight played against the great veins of quartz, revealing all the colors of a prism. The sparkling lights were mesmerizing. It was like being surrounded by a most beautiful rainbow, and it occurred to Michael that even if dozens of prospectors had already entered this magical place, they had probably not fully realized the relationship between quartz and gold. That being the case, it would never have occurred to them to work the rock walls high above.

"So how do I get up there?" he asked himself, because the lowest exposed vein of quartz was a good twenty feet overhead.

Michael thought it over for at least an hour and then he decided that he would have to chop down a couple of lodgepole pines and use strips of his blankets to bind them together, ladder fashion. That decided, Michael spent a full day cutting down two pines, laboriously hauling them into the fissure and propping them up against the narrow walls.

It pained him greatly to fashion strips from one of his three thin blankets but he was not about to use his coat or the leather from his boots. By evening, he had his pine ladder reaching well above the lowest ledge of quartz.

That night it rained, and Michael was grateful for the rock overhang as he stared into his fire and chewed beef jerky, washing it down with icy riverwater.

Early in November, 1851

My Beloved Miss Tessa:

I am writing in my diary now because I am out of letter paper and envelopes and haven't the dollar for postage even if there were someone about that I dared entrust to deliver a letter. I am as alone as a man could ever be. There may not be another human being within ten miles and the walls of my little rock prison rise up so steeply that I see only a sliver of a starry heaven. I miss you terribly and I miss Paddy too, but I think he was right to leave. It has been, if anything, a harder existence since he left me. I have cut myself off from the "herd" and struck off on my own, knowing at last that it is my only hope. Tomorrow I will crawl upon a pole ladder and attack the outcroppings of quartz high above. If I break enough of it free, I might find an entire vein of gold, according to a geologist I heard speak in Columbia.

On the other hand, my ladder might break under my weight and I could fall to my death, in which case my bones would not be found until next spring—if then. That is why I write to you now despite the weariness I feel. I know that, at this very hour, you are thinking of me and praying for my return because not even the distance of the universe could separate our thoughts or dilute the power of our love. So then, tomorrow I will try something new, certain that the quartz deposits directly over my head have never felt a prospector's pick or hammer. Mine will be the first and I pray that it will yield the fortune that I have long promised and which will at last deliver me to your side.

Your devoted fiancé,
MICHAEL W. CALLAHAN, Esq.

When Michael awoke in the morning, a cold, misting rain was still filtering out of a leaden sky. His fire, though protected and dry, was low and he was stiff from the previous day's heavy work of dragging, lifting and then positioning the lodgepoles against the fissure wall. Furthermore, Michael was almost weak from hunger. His supplies were meager but he cooked a half pound of salt pork and a couple of potatoes. He had no coffee or tea so he washed his food down with hot water from a tin cup.

By ten o'clock, the expectancy and restlessness in him was so great that he could not wait for the weather to improve. Buttoning his collar under his chin, he crawled out from under his rock shelf and gripped one of the pines. He shook it hard, loosening a great shower of water.

Shoving his axe in one coat pocket and his rock pick in another, he scaled the wet, shaky ladder certain that the soggy blanket strips that bound everything together were going to tear free and send him falling to his death on the rock floor below. But they held, and he was able to reach the vein of quartz after a quarter hour of scooting his way upward.

At the top, the pines were no more than eight inches in diameter, and every time Michael swung his rock hammer the trees would shake and he would almost topple. It was hard, dangerous work but he was grimly determined not to quit until he had dislodged a ton of quartz or exposed a vein of pure gold.

By noon he was so exhausted that he could barely raise the hammer to strike the quartz, but the drizzling rain had been replaced by the sun, which quickly warmed the day so that his soggy coat began to steam.

Michael's eyes ached for the sight of gold. Below him lay a big pile of scattered quartz. Struggling with fear, fatigue and disappointment, Michael inched a little higher until he was lying flat on the very tip of one log and hugging the other while trying to flail away with his hammer. It was brutally exhausting work and he was sure he would fall to his death with every swing of his hammer.

"Enough," he finally whispered as he was gasping for breath and hugging the soggy bark of his tree.

It took him ten minutes to inch back down the slippery pine, and he ripped his coat in the process. Crawling on the ground, Michael pulled a large hunk of broken quartz to his side and raised it to the sun above. He turned the quartz this way and that before his eyes widened in amazement and he began to shake like a wet dog.

"Could it be?" he whispered, staring at the flecks of gold. "Could it really be?"

It *was* gold! For ten frenzied minutes he pulverized the quartz with his hammer until he had broken away flakes and chunks of gold—enough to fill a teaspoon from a single large rock. Enough to bring him twenty, maybe twenty-five dollars.

"Eureka!" he screamed, rolling over on his back and laughing almost hysterically to the wedge of blue sky above. "Eureka, I have found it!"

Winter, 1851

My Beloved Miss Tessa:

Forgive me for not writing for so long but I have been working so hard that I have not had either time nor strength to do anything but extract gold from the quartz. I have stayed at this place in the high mountains too long. Now I am near starvation. I will die if I remain here any longer without food or shelter other than these rocks and what little remains of rabbit and fowl I have trapped down by the Stanislaus River. But most important of all, I am leaving for help with no less than five thousand dollars worth of gold in my pack. All evidence of my stay—including several tons of broken quartz—have been dumped in the river and I will wipe out my own tracks with a branch of pine.

In the springtime, I will return from Hangtown with Paddy and we will become rich because the vein I have found has not yet been exhausted. Pray for me that I can reach help in time.

Your devoted fiancé,

MICHAEL W. CALLAHAN, Esq.

Michael shouldered his heavy pack, staggering under its weight. There was at least five thousand dollars' worth of gold in his pack and he would get it down to civilization even if he had to crawl.

When satisfied his tracks were wiped clean, he took one last glance back at his fissure of rock, then struggled down the river trail. This should have been one of the happiest moments of his life, but he was so thin and weak that he might actually fall and be unable to get up again. And no one would find him way up here in this uninhabited canyon in the middle of winter. The footing was treacherous and, because the tread had worn off the soles of his boots, he kept slipping and falling. Each time, he managed to rise again and push on.

Michael lost track of time. Sometimes he grew dizzy and forgot which direction he should follow. Then he would remember to follow the powerful, snow-fed Stanislaus.

That first night, he stumbled into a Chinese camp, and they fed him cooked vegetables, though he begged and offered to pay them well for meat. But the Orientals had no meat, so he ate their strange fare which could not satisfy his hunger. They gave him two extra blankets and hot tea until he was overcome by sleep.

In the morning Michael continued, after giving the Chinese his gold pan in repayment for their great kindness. They seemed very pleased. That second afternoon, he came upon another camp tended by three surly men who watched him stumble in and nearly collapse by their fire.

"Food," Michael gasped. "I need food."

"We all need food," the largest of the men rumbled. "You got money for it?"

Michael had no choice but to fumble in his pack until he produced a palmful of shiny gold nuggets.

"Holy cow!" one of the prospectors exclaimed. "What'd you do, make a strike?"

"No!" Michael looked away, knowing his lie was childishly transparent. "Yes," Michael whispered, "now, please, food!"

The large man grabbed for Michael's pack and he didn't have the strength to keep it out of the stranger's grasp. "That's mine!"

"Would you look at this!" the man exclaimed. "We're rich!"

Michael had no gun, only an axe and a knife. He drew the knife from his belt and came to his feet. "Give it back!"

But the big man just pulled his gun. "Mister," he hissed, "say your prayers."

"Wait!" one of them objected. "If there's a bullet in him, they'll know it was us! Ain't nobody else up here."

"What about that greaser camp a mile below?"

"Yeah," the third man said, "we could say it was the Mexicans. Probably have to stab him, though."

Michael began to inch backward toward the river as they plotted his demise.

"Stab, shoot, what's the difference?" one of them groused. "Nobody can prove nothin'!"

When Michael felt the water licking at his ankles, he turned and threw himself headlong into the current. The water was so cold it seemed to wring the blood from his bones. He was torn under the surface and sent spinning into a freezing darkness.

His shoulder struck a submerged rock and when he could hold his breath not a second more, the river tossed him upward and he broke through the water wolfing in deep breaths and clawing toward the shore like a wild animal. Michael was swept around a bend and carried another mile before he touched the riverbed and dragged himself from the water. He heard shouts. Unable to move much and shaking violently from the cold, he twisted around, certain that the prospectors had overtaken him and that they were about to bury a knife in his throat.

"Ha!" a man said with only a slight Spanish accent. "You are the one who tried to help my friends. They call you the Gringo Amigo."

Teeth chattering violently, Michael looked up to see a handsome vaquero. "Joaquín!" he blurted. "Please. Half my gold if you can get it from the camp above!"

Joaquín frowned. He rolled a cigarette and lit it with a match that he struck on one of the coins sewn into the seam of his pants. "How much, señor?"

"Five thousand," he said through chattering teeth. "At least."

Joaquín had started to suck on his smoke but his hand stopped midway to his lips. "Madre mia! Where did you find this gold?"

Michael swallowed. "I can't tell you."

Now Joaquín smoked. "Then I take all the five thousand but I help you to live so you can go back. Comprende?"

Michael clenched his bloodless fists together. He wanted to scream in helpless frustration. After all the sacrifice, to have to give all his gold away was nearly more than he could bear. "Agreed!"

Joaquín called out in Spanish and moments later Michael felt himself being lifted and carried into the camp. He was laid inside a tent where a big Mexican woman tore off his wet clothes, covered him with a warm, dry blanket and began rubbing it vigorously against his thin body to generate heat.

"Gracias, señora!"

"Sí, Gringo Amigo."

Michael looked back out through the tent and saw the magnificent Joaquín on horseback followed by several other vaqueros as they spurred their horses upriver.

"I hope they will kill all three," Michael swore through his chattering teeth.

In reply, the fat old Mexican woman threw her brown eyes heavenward and made the sign of the cross.

Five

JOAQUÍN MURIETA eased himself down in a chair beside Michael's bed and cocked one leg over his knee, then fiddled absently with his big-roweled spurs.

"Gringo, you have been very sick for a long time. So how are you feeling today?"

"Weak and tired. How long did I have the fever?"

Joaquín shrugged. He was not dressed so fine now as he had been that Sunday morning in Columbia. Instead of the silver-lined jacket with its intricate embroidery work, he wore a heavy wool serape and his pants were stained and made of leather. He smelled of horse and sweat and his cheeks were covered with a two-day stubble. Even so, he was still a strikingly handsome man.

"I did not keep count of the days that you were crazy. And even afterward, you slept for a long time."

"Where am I?"

"This cabin belongs to Señora Gómez."

"And she has been with me all this time?"

"And others."

"Then I owe you all my life."

A slow smile crossed Joaquín's lips. "Five thousand dollars in gold is handsome pay for anyone's life, señor."

A coughing spell seized Michael so powerfully that it felt as if spikes were being driven into his lungs. He had to struggle for every breath, and he was so weak that the coughing left him completely drained.

"Amigo," Joaquín said with concern, "I have more bad news for you."

"What else could happen?"

"Your claim. My people have found its gold."

"What!" Michael tried to sit up, but his excitement caused him to have another coughing spell and when Joaquín gently pushed him back down on the bed he did not have the strength to resist.

"Listen, señor. The Mexican people are suffering at the hands of your people. Women and children are starving, and the men are being lynched if they do not give up their rightful claims. The money was needed to help them."

"But I gave you five thousand dollars! The claim was supposed to be mine!"

Joaquín sighed heavily. "I know, and it makes me very ashamed to admit that I was the one that discovered your claim and told my people about the quartz rock on the walls."

Michael groaned, causing Joaquín to lift up his hands and drop them to his lap in resignation. "All right, señor, I admit that I am a thief and a terrible person. Everyone knows that Joaquín Murieta is no good. But I thought you would die and would have no need of your claim."

"You have no idea how much I needed that gold," Michael choked. "I promised my love I would return rich."

At this piece of news, Joaquín brightened. "Amigo!" he exclaimed. "If it is just for a woman, then do not feel so bad! After all, there is always more women and more gold. You will find both."

But Michael was disconsolate, and he shook his head back and forth. "I don't have the strength or the heart for it."

"But you will! So open your eyes and look at me."

Michael looked and now saw that Joaquín's expression was very serious. "Amigo! You have *life*. This is the most important thing. And also you have dignity. This is very important too."

"What dignity? I have less than when I arrived in California. Look at me! I have nothing!"

Joaquín dropped his boot to the rough plank floor with a loud thud. He stood up and began to pace back and forth, his rowels singing against the wood. "Gringo Amigo, I will give you a gun, a fine horse and a good saddle. How would that be?"

"It would be a start," Michael said without much enthusiasm. "I could sell the horse and saddle for another stake."

Joaquín recoiled in outrage. "Sell the horse! So what would you ride, señor?"

"I would walk."

Joaquín scoffed. "Walking is for peasants and farmers. Do you know how to ride?"

"No. I was raised in a city."

"Ah! So that is it! Then I will teach you to ride."

Joaquín folded his arms across his chest. He eyed Michael with great skepticism. "Can you shoot a gun?"

"Not well. I never owned a rifle or pistol."

Shaking his head, Joaquín rolled his eyes toward the ceiling. "In this country, a man needs a horse, a gun and a good woman —but not necessarily in that order. No?"

"I guess not."

"Of course not. Without a woman to love, what is life, señor?"

Michael thought of his Tessa. "Nothing."

"This is true! And you have nothing, so no wonder you are sick in body and spirit."

"Maybe I do need a horse and gun. But not a woman. The one I love waits for me in New York City."

"But that is so far! No?"

"Yes."

"Amigo, the women in California are very beautiful. I could introduce you to many, even if you are a gringo."

"No, thank you."

Joaquín scowled. "Why doesn't your woman come here?"

"Because a poor woman's life is too hard in the gold fields."

"Life is hard anywhere for the woman of a poor man. But with love . . ." Joaquín winked. "Do you want to see my woman?" The vaquero so obviously desired to introduce his woman that Michael nodded his head. Joaquín rushed out of the little cabin, reappearing a few minutes later with the same beautiful young señorita that they had first seen bantering with Joaquín on the streets of Columbia last year. "This is *my* woman," Joaquín announced with pride. "Señorita Rosita Sánchez, meet the Gringo Amigo."

Michael fidgeted a little subconsciously when the woman extended her hand, aware that his face would bear a long scab from the bullet he had taken across his cheek and his eyes were probably dark with suffering and fever.

"Señorita Sánchez, it is an honor."

Her English was not good, but after Joaquín had translated, Rosita smiled and appeared very pleased. She said something to Joaquín and they both laughed.

"What is so funny?"

"She says you are the tall one who stared at her breasts in Columbia as if you had never before seen a pair on a woman."

Michael blushed deeply. "I . . . I apologize," he managed to say.

"Por nada, it is nothing," Joaquín said, waving his hand. "So what will you do now?"

"I don't know," Michael admitted. "As soon as I am strong enough to leave, I will do so. I have been here too long already."

"Where will you go?"

"Hangtown," Michael said without thinking. "I . . . I have a friend there."

"You have friends here. Never before has a gringo stood beside us against his own people to right a great injustice. Your reputation is already great among my people. You are the Gringo Amigo to us now."

"But I saved no lives. I was not even as brave as I was afraid."

"A man can have courage and also good sense," Joaquín reasoned. "It is no shame to save your life so that you can fight another day. You should stay with us, señor. We can work together."

Michael shook his head. "I would make a poor vaquero."

"As I make a poor prospector," Joaquín admitted. "But we can both learn, no?"

"Maybe."

Rosita said something in Spanish. Her dark eyes never left Michael's face and he asked, "What did she say?"

Joaquín winked. "Rosita says that the path of the bullet across your face makes you very, very handsome."

Michael's hand involuntarily touched his face. He was shocked to feel not a scab, but a long groove across his cheek.

"I was never handsome before. I can't be tricked into thinking that I am now."

When Joaquín translated his words into Spanish, Rosita laughed as loud and as naturally as a man. She leaned close to Joaquín and giggled something, then left them to walk outside, her hips swaying provocatively.

Joaquín clucked his tongue. "That one would make any man forget past promises," he said. "And I know a young woman named Aurora López that has the same kind of fire. After I teach you to ride a horse, we could go over to Hornitos and see her sometime, eh, señor?"

Michael tore his eyes from the departing girl, feeling guilty that he had even admired another woman. "No," he said quickly. "I don't think so. Find a young vaquero like yourself."

Joaquín laughed at Michael's embarrassment. But, in truth, it was a nice laugh, not at all offensive, and it made Michael smile in spite of his own discomfort.

Two weeks later Michael was dressed in a pair of boots and riding pants and presented with a pair of Mexican spurs. The spurs weren't fancy and of engraved silver like Joaquín's, but they were quite beautiful and had leather straps tooled in a pretty floral design.

"Joaquín, I don't think I need these," he protested. "I don't want a horse to do anything but walk."

"Put the spurs on, Amigo. You don't know what you need."

Michael did as he was told. When he walked around the cabin, the spurs jingled just like Joaquín's and, in spite of his apprehension, he liked their sound and feel.

"Come outside to meet your new caballo, Amigo!"

Michael followed the vaquero outside. He knew that Joaquín had been hunting for just the right animal for the past two weeks and was almost as excited as himself. Because the vaquero had a discerning eye for both beautiful horses and a beautiful woman, Michael suspected that the gift he was about to receive would be special. He was not disappointed. Even Rosita, who held the animal, could not distract Michael's attention from the magnificent sorrel with its flaxen mane and tail.

"She's beautiful!" Michael blurted.

"Yes," Joaquín said with a twinkle in his dark eyes, "and so is the gelding, no?"

"Oh . . . yes, of course!" Michael blushed with embarrassment. *"He* is a fine animal."

"Then we will go for a ride."

Michael's smile faded. "Uh . . . shouldn't I . . ."

"What?"

"Well, get acquainted a little. You know, feed him or something so that we become friends."

Joaquín had trouble suppressing his laughter, and several other vaqueros who were standing by to watch chortled softly.

Anger flashed in Michael's eyes. "Now listen," he said, "I'm not in any hurry to get thrown for your amusement. And that horse looks very spirited."

"Oh," Joaquín said quite seriously, "he is!"

"Maybe a little *too* spirited."

In answer Joaquín stepped over to Rosita, took the animal's reins from her hands, grabbed the saddle horn and swung onto the sorrel's back. He whirled the horse around and touched its sleek flanks with his spurs and the gelding's hooves cupped and hurled dirt at them as it exploded into a run.

Michael watched openmouthed as the vaquero raced the horse across the meadow, then reined it hard, sending the horse skidding across the grass on its rear hocks, only to spin about again and come charging for the cabin.

Michael swallowed and thought to himself: *If I lived a thousand years, I could never ride like that.*

As Joaquín raced back toward the yard, a chicken shot out from under the cabin and the vaquero, without using his reins, guided the sorrel with his legs as he chased the squawking fowl down, bent low against the gelding's side and snatched the chicken up by its neck, ending forever its cackling protest.

Señora Gómez suddenly appeared from around the back of her cabin, and even though Michael did not know much Spanish, he could tell that the old Mexican woman was giving the vaquero a strong piece of her mind for throttling one of her chickens.

Joaquín pulled the sorrel to a standstill, and even though it was trembling with excitement he dropped the reins on its neck and the horse did not move. Joaquín swept off his sombrero and made a very sincere apology to Señora Gómez before he threw a leg over his off-stirrup, then gracefully slid down to present the dead chicken to the woman with a low bow.

Señora Gómez could not maintain her anger, and when she smiled, it broke the tension, causing all the Mexicans to laugh and hoot.

"Now," Joaquín said, turning to Michael, "it is *your* turn. This horse will not hurt you. I know this in my heart."

Michael made an awkward show of climbing onto the saddle. When he managed to get both boots into his stirrups, he realized that a horse was much taller when you were on its back than when you were standing beside it.

"What do I do now?"

"We go," Joaquín said, striding over to his own animal. "And when we return, you will know how to ride."

"I wish that I could believe it was that simple."

"It *is* simple if you think it is simple," Joaquín said, reining his horse around and beckoning Michael to follow.

They walked out into the meadow, Michael just getting the feel of a horse between his legs. The sorrel was tossing its head a little and Joaquín said, "He has a very soft mouth, Amigo. You must be very gentle with your reins. And you must relax. Draw back your shoulders with pride, like a vaquero. Smell the pines and let the sun warm your cheeks and give them some color."

Michael made a conscious effort to relax. The rocking motion of the horse was very soothing, and after they had walked almost a mile he felt much better.

"Now," Joaquín said, "first the trot."

He showed Michael how to make the sorrel trot, but not run. The trot was terrible. It made Michael's brain beat against the inside of his skull and it drove his spine into his butt.

"I don't like the trot!"

"You must learn to enjoy it by leaning forward a little and putting some of your weight on your legs, feet and stirrups. The trot is very important."

"Why?"

"Because it is easy on a horse if the rider does not bounce or stay too far back. A horse can trot for hours. It is the fastest way to travel a long distance."

Michael didn't think he could have trotted another fifty yards.

"Now the gallop."

"Couldn't we wait until next time?"

"No."

So they galloped side by side, stirrup to stirrup. Michael tried to grab his saddle horn, but Joaquín reached out and tore his hand from it.

"Well, what the hell is it for if not to grab on to?"

"It is for a reata," Joaquín said in a way that brooked no argument.

Somehow Michael did hold on, and when they slowed their mounts back to a walk he felt well pleased with himself and was sure that his friend would be very impressed. "What do you think?"

"I think," Joaquín said, rolling a cigarette with his slender, supple fingers, "that you will always ride like a gringo."

"You're insulting me."

"Sí." Joaquín finished rolling his smoke and lighting it. He exhaled through his nostrils. "But you will learn, Amigo. Give yourself a little time and you will learn."

"I haven't got much time. I need to make another gold strike."

"First you need to learn to ride this horse and shoot a gun and a rifle."

Michael started to protest, but then he thought about the three men who had almost killed him upriver and he knew that Joaquín was right.

"When will we start?"

"As soon as this riding is over," Joaquín said, reaching back to his saddlebags and producing a handsome pistol, holster and cartridge belt.

The belt was a little loose but Michael did not care. The pistol was the same sort of Colt percussion revolver that he'd seen men carrying all over the gold fields.

"It won't go off suddenly now, will it?"

"No. It is not loaded yet."

"Good," Michael said. "If I accidentally shoot myself in the leg, I'll never get to Hangtown this year."

Joaquín said nothing, but he didn't have to. He'd already asked Michael to stay in the Mexican camp until late in the spring and then they, together, would find more gold.

FOR TWO MORE WEEKS, Michael and Joaquín rode horses every day. Their rides grew increasingly longer and more challenging, until they were galloping easily and jumping small streams and fallen trees. Joaquín taught Michael how best to distribute his weight over the sorrel's withers when making a steep climb up a mountainside, and how to take care of the horse both before and after it was saddled.

They also practiced with the pistols and a rifle. As with horses, Joaquín was expert with firearms. "You must not jerk the trigger but gently squeeze and caress it like you would a piece of fruit or the breasts of a beautiful woman."

The analogy embarrassed Michael and he supposed that was exactly the reason Joaquín used it. During their time together, it became apparent to Michael that, while Joaquín was a good and generous man, he was also moody and possessed a devilish streak. Michael never saw Joaquín lose his temper, but he was sure the vaquero had a dangerous side. He had also never dared to ask the vaquero what had become of the three men who had tried to kill him for his gold, because he knew the answer. Joaquín, for all his charm and easy laughter, was not the sort of man who did things in half measures. If he loved, it was with all his heart, and if he hated, God help his enemies.

When the snow was gone and flowers were blooming in the meadow and on the mountainsides, Michael wrote a letter to Tessa.

Spring, 1852

My Beloved Miss Tessa:

All winter I have been writing in my diary whose pages I yearn to share with you after we are wed. Until now, I have been living in a community of Mexicans on the upper reaches of the Stanislaus. My good vaquero friend, Joaquín Murieta, as well as the others here, refer to me as "The Gringo Amigo" because I almost got myself killed trying to protect their mining claim last fall.

Now, I am learning to ride a horse and shoot guns and rifles so that I can fight with a better chance of survival. I have often fought with my fists, but things are different in the gold camps. Here, life has very little value among the ruffians and thieves, or even, for that matter, among men like Joaquín who obviously do not fear death so much as humiliation and the loss of dignity.

I have been sick for a long time but I am getting strong again, thanks to these good and happy people. Joaquín, who is a vaquero, is trying to learn to become a prospector. This is sad, really, but he tells me that the grand ranchos are all being divided into small farms and ranchos by the gringos who take the land from the Mexican and Spanish grantees. The Mexicans hate both the Greaser's Act and the Foreign Miner's Tax which were passed by the new California government to deliberately rob them and the Chinese of their mining claims.

In addition to shooting practice, and daily riding my new horse that I named "Nugget," I have been learning some Spanish and teaching these people a little English. Now, I am going to Hangtown to see Paddy Ryan. I think I have at last found the secret to finding a gold strike. In fact, I am sure I have the secret and hope to lure Paddy back to the hills.

I will write again before posting this letter in Hangtown.

Your devoted fiancé,

MICHAEL W. CALLAHAN, Esq.

Michael read and reread the letter several times that evening. He had decided to omit telling Tessa about his strike and how it had been lost to thieves and then his Mexican friends. Tessa, he was sure, would not understand and it would be futile even to attempt to explain in a letter how his friends could take his five thousand dollars in gold and steal his claim. It was, at times, difficult even for himself to understand. All Michael knew for certain was that these good people had saved his life.

In truth, he was no longer upset about the loss of his gold. Michael knew that he could discover more quartz and that, when he did, he would also find more gold.

The next morning, Rosita and Señora Gómez gave him hugs, kisses on his scarred cheek and more food than he could possibly eat on the road to Hangtown.

"Come back soon, Amigo," Joaquín said, looking sad to see

his friend go away. "Because I taught you how to ride a horse and shoot straight, you can teach me to find more gold. We could be partners."

"What about Rosita?"

Joaquín barked a laugh. "With you I share *gold,* never women."

"I know that," Michael said. "I was just seeing if I could—for once—get your goat as you so often do mine."

Joaquín, realizing that he had been tricked, was greatly amused and the sadness left his face. "You come back. I'll introduce you to the beautiful Señorita Aurora López."

"How come I have never seen her in Sonora?"

"She lives in Hornitos," Joaquín said, with a wink. "It is a long ride—but worth it."

Michael shook hands with his friend and mounted the sorrel. "Will you stay at this claim?"

"I don't think so," Joaquín said. "We must move on. There is no gold left up here."

Michael's opinion was very much the same. "Then where?"

Joaquín shrugged his shoulders. "You will find us if you want."

It was true. "Adios," Michael said.

At the edge of the meadow, he sharply reined his gelding around and waved at the Mexican camp. Joaquín, Rosita and the others all waved back.

"Adios, my friends," Michael whispered as he turned the sorrel north and galloped off toward Hangtown.

Six

JUST AS IN EARLY SPRING when the snow-fed rivers rushed down the western slopes of the Sierra Nevada Mountains, so too did the eager prospectors return to the gold fields after wintering in California's warm Central Valley. Michael rode through towns churning with an onslaught of fresh gold-seekers. Heavy rains had filled the streets until they became gutters of mud but that did not faze the onslaught of prospectors bound for the gold fields.

On his way to Hangtown, Michael saw two gold strikes explode into life right before his eyes. It took little more than the drunken shout "Gold at Red Dog Gulch!" to stampede the miners off to another frenzied camp where little squares of river or stream would be bid up into the thousands of dollars.

From atop his fine horse, Nugget, Michael now witnessed a more lofty and detached perspective of life in the California gold fields. No longer did his pulse race whenever he heard of a new strike. In fact, as he sat atop Nugget and watched the miners grab their pans, packs and picks to sprint away with a fresh burst of gold fever, Michael felt a little pity, knowing from firsthand experience that only about one out of a thousand prospectors would really make a strike.

"Why don't you join 'em?" an old man on crutches demanded from the porch of the Bonanza Hotel in Angel's Camp only moments after the rumors of another new strike had emptied the town.

"I just don't think they'll find anything," Michael reasoned from atop his horse.

The old man's eyebrows knitted with disapproval. "Why, if I had a horse like that and I was young like you, I'd be a-racin' off to beat them other fellas out! I'd be one of the first to arrive and I'd stake my claim and get rich every time there was a new strike."

"You'd try," Michael said. "In my opinion, by the time the word spreads, all the good claims are already filed and the late-comers wind up with nothing."

"Humph! You got a fancy horse, clothes, saddle and money," the old man said, wobbling anxiously about on his crutches and looking for all the world as if he were about to take a flying leap off the porch and head out after the stampeding miners, "but most of them boys that took off for Red Dog Gulch are broke and half-starved."

"And they always will be chasing strikes like that," Michael commented with a shake of his head.

"Humph!" the man snorted again before he banged his crutches down on the porch floor and disappeared into the deserted hotel.

Several hours later when he rode into Angel's Camp, Michael made the happy discovery of gold dust hidden in his saddlebags under tortillas and beef jerky packed by Joaquín himself.

Michael's spirits took wing. "Thank you, amigo," he said. "I was wondering how I was going to buy grain for Nugget and pay for my room and board tonight."

Michael judged there to be about seven ounces of gold in the poke. Once again, he found himself unable to comprehend how his Mexican friend could take his money and his claim without any sense of guilt or remorse and then be so generous even though he and his people were struggling for their very existence. Mexicans, he reasoned, sure looked at things with a different perspective.

That night it rained hard in Angel's Camp, but that didn't dampen the miners from their hell-raising. There was a shooting in the street right beneath Michael's hotel window around midnight and although he didn't go down to investigate, he heard men shouting—first for the doctor, then the undertaker. Early the next morning, Michael ordered a breakfast of bacon and eggs, coffee and bread that cost him sixteen dollars and left him shaking his head.

"At these prices," he said to the cafe owner before departing, "it's easy to see who is making all the money off this gold rush."

"You try bringing up fresh eggs from Stockton," the man groused. "Half of them will get busted before they arrive and most of those that don't break will get eaten on the trail. They cost me a dollar apiece by the time they arrive. You want to bring up a couple hundred dozen, go ahead and try."

"No, thanks," Michael said, thoroughly chastised. "How far to Hangtown?"

"Better'n forty miles, I 'spect."

"Thanks," Michael said on his way out.

The day was overcast and drizzling rain as he rode up through the busy gold camps of San Andreas, Mokelumne Hill, Jackson and Sutter Creek, where nothing remained of Sutter's sawmill where the Forty-Niner Gold Rush had all begun. Michael trotted through El Dorado, and late afternoon found him entering Hangtown.

His first impression of Hangtown was not favorable. The streets were crowded and knee-deep in mud. Michael was forced to rein Nugget around discarded boots and clothes, empty wooden crates, rusting tin cans of every size and description, worn-out pots and pans, bones, bottles and about everything else imaginable in the muddy road leading into Hangtown's business district.

Perhaps most unusual of all was the sight of miners actually digging up the street itself in the search for gold. Every few hundred feet Michael would come upon a group of miners, usually one digging, one bailing muddy water out of the hole and another standing on a soggy mud heap pitching shovelfuls of mud into a rocker. Prospecting right in the middle of the street created an especially large headache for the struggling freight wagons and there was much shouting and cursing.

From travelers going south that Michael had met, he learned that Hangtown had originally been called "Old Dry Diggin's" and, in July of '48, had been the site of a huge gold discovery. Seventeen thousand dollars' worth of placer gold had been found in one week and soon the area had been overrun with feverish miners.

Every gold strike brought both good men and bad and Old Dry Diggin's, which had changed its name to Ravine City, had more than its share of the latter. A small army of claim jumpers and outlaws formed a loose confederation called "The Owls" and they robbed and murdered for gold every night. Finally a vigilante committee was formed, and one night after a Frenchman was robbed of fifty ounces of dust, they went into action. After quickly overtaking the three thieves, they gave the Owls a quick trial and then strung them up from the bough of a great oak tree that stood at the corner of Main and Coloma streets. The hanging served notice to the other Owls, but some were slow learners and many more like "Irish Dick" Crone and Bill Brown jigged their way to hell before the bad element fled and Ravine City became known as Hangtown.

Now, as Michael rode into the soggy settlement, he was surprised to see that it had a permanent population of over three thousand. Michael followed winding Hangtown Creek up to Main Street, which was intersected by dozens of narrow streets crowded by clapboarded houses and businesses. He was looking for Potter's general store.

"There's a big one about a block up and on your right," a man in a red-checkered shirt yelled from the seat of a freight wagon.

"Much obliged."

"Say, want to sell that handsome sorrel?"

"No, sir."

"Give you a hundred dollars in dust!"

"No, thanks."

"You might change your mind after you see what it's gonna cost you for hay."

Michael supposed that he was in for a shock. He could read the advertising signs along the streets, and the prices of everything were outrageous.

Haircuts were five dollars. Shaves, two dollars. Beer a dollar a bottle, and a steak with a potato, bread and coffee cost thirty dollars. A tin of sardines was four dollars, and a pickle was six bits. From these prices, Michael supposed that a bale of hay hauled up from the Central Valley would be at least twenty dollars and Nugget would devour one every four days.

"Gonna have to get Paddy out of here in a hurry or we'll both starve," Michael said, patting Nugget on the shoulder as he reined him around a busted wagon wheel half-buried in mud.

Michael had expected to find a store named Potter's Emporium, like the original dry goods store in Mariposa that Mr. Potter had opened and run so successfully. Instead, he grinned to see PADDY'S EMPORIUM stenciled in large white letters.

"Well I'll be damned," he exclaimed, reining up Nugget and admiring the sign. "Looks like Paddy is doing all right for himself."

Michael dismounted with relief. His pants were rain-soaked and his legs were raw from the unaccustomed long hours in the saddle. He tied the sorrel to a hitch post in front of the store, then mounted the porch, his spurs jingling like a real vaquero's and his cheeks covered with a two-day stubble of beard. He scraped as much mud as he could from the soles of his riding boots, then removed his battered old hat and entered the general store.

The first thing he saw was a plump but pretty young woman standing behind the counter with a smile. "Can I help you find something?"

Michael glanced around for a moment, taking in the smells and the sight. It was a real nice business. "Yes, ma'am," he said. "I'm lookin' for Paddy Ryan. He works here."

"Yes, he does," she said sweetly. "I'm *Mrs.* Ryan and we own this store."

Michael's jaw dropped with surprise and he must have looked like a gaping idiot because the woman's smile died on her lips and she asked with concern, "Is something wrong?"

"Well . . . well, no, ma'am! It's just that I . . . well, I'll be jingoed! Here I am figuring to lure my best friend back into the gold fields, but now I discover that he not only owns this place, but he's won himself a pretty young wife."

The woman managed to smile again, though it was plain she wasn't too sure about Michael. "You say you're his best friend?"

"That's right!" Michael stuck out his calloused hand and told the woman his name.

"You're Michael Callahan!"

"I am."

"I'm Pearl," she said, smiling warmly now. "And Paddy has told me about you dozens of times. He said that you'd come sauntering in here one day. But you don't seem at all like he described."

"Hard luck changes a man," Michael said, wondering how much the prominent scar on his cheek was throwing this woman off.

"Can I get you some coffee and something to eat?" she said quickly. "You look tired and hungry, Mr. Callahan."

"Michael," he said.

"All right. Then you must call me Pearl."

He nodded. "Paddy around?"

"He had to make a quick trip to Sacramento yesterday, but he'll be back by this evening. Did you know that he's been elected to our city council?"

"Already?" Michael shook his head. "It was only last fall that he and I separated. Less than a year. Now he's married, owns a store and is a councilman? Boy howdy, he's really made some progress in a hurry."

Pearl came around the counter and touched Michael's coat. "Paddy still talks about you constantly."

"Then he must have told you that I am engaged to marry a lady named Tessa Glynn just as soon as I strike it rich and return to New York City."

"Yes, he did," Pearl said. "I'm sure she is a beautiful young lady."

"So are you, Mrs. Ryan."

Pearl beamed, and that made her look even prettier. She was a little on the stout side, but her cheeks were rosy and her smile warmed a man's heart. Michael had liked Pearl from the very first moment.

"Sit down over here," she said, beckoning him to the chair beside the counter. "Fish yourself out some pickles and crackers. Take all you want."

"I'd rather stand," Michael said, noting the prices posted on the pickle and cracker barrel. "And I'm not too hungry. Just ate dinner."

"Where?"

She had him. He was starving, and he hadn't eaten since breakfast. "Uh . . . I forgot the name."

Pearl seemed to look right through him. She used a long fork to stab a pickle and then she scooped up a handful of crackers. "Beer or a soda?"

"Beer."

In a moment she had him munching away while she told him all about how her father had opened the store last year but her mother had detested Hangtown.

"It was busy and violent," Pearl explained, "so she and my father returned to Mariposa. I'd already fallen in love with Paddy and he—thank the Lord—also fell in love with me. We were married on Christmas Day. The church bells were tolling happily, and it was all very beautiful. Now we live right upstairs, but Paddy has promised we'll build a nice house just as soon as the business grows a little more."

"It looks like it's already well on its way."

"It is," Pearl said. "My father said that Paddy is a natural storekeeper. He likes to talk to the customers and everybody loves him. That's why they asked him to run for the city council."

Pearl leaned forward and whispered, "Everyone says my husband will be mayor next. And they say that someday he will go into state politics."

The woman was so proud and excited that Michael completely forgot his own disappointment that Paddy would not be joining him in the gold fields, this spring or any other spring. It seemed pretty obvious that he'd found a gold mine right here on Main Street.

They talked for almost an hour before Michael excused himself. "I need to find a stable and put my horse up. Then I'd like to find a room with a bath. I need to shave."

"Your best bet is the Hangtown Livery. Tell old Caleb that you're Paddy's best friend. He'll treat you fairly and your horse will get the best of care."

"I'll do that," Michael promised.

"And after you've gotten that room and cleaned up, come on back. I'll be closing the store at five and we'll have plenty more time to visit after Paddy comes home."

Michael went back outside and mounted his horse. Pearl, standing in the doorway, said, "My but she's a beautiful animal!"

"It's a *he,*" Michael corrected, smiling inwardly to remember making the exact same mistake the first time he'd set his eyes on Nugget.

"Paddy never told me you were such a fine horseman," Pearl said as Michael reined the gelding about just as though he'd been doing it from infancy.

"Well, Pearl, if the truth be known," Michael called, "I'm not all that good yet. Not near like a cowboy or a vaquero. But I do enjoy riding a whole lot more than walking."

"I sure hope so," Pearl called, "because even if you are Paddy's best friend, you're going to pay a little fortune to keep that animal fat in this town."

Michael nodded, his smile evaporating and then he reined

Nugget on down the muddy street toward the Hangtown Livery.

Two hours later and two ounces of gold dust lighter, Michael finished dressing. He had shaved and bathed, put on a clean shirt and pants, and he guessed he was about as presentable as he could ever be. It was nearly sundown. His stomach was grumbling. He figured that, at the prices of a room and a stall in Hangtown, he could afford to remain about one more day, perhaps two, before he spent the last of his gold dust. It was a mighty good thing that Paddy wasn't visiting San Francisco.

When Michael arrived back on Main Street, Paddy was waiting anxiously outside his store. Fifty pounds heavier, dressed in a dark-brown suit, wearing muttonchop whiskers and a big gold watch and chain, he looked every inch a prosperous young merchant. Michael would hardly have recognized him from the thin, irritable fellow he'd last seen at Whiskey Slide.

"Mike?" Paddy asked, equally surprised by his best friend's gaunt and haggard appearance and the prominent bullet scar on his cheek.

"Yeah, it's me."

"Holy Jaysus!" Paddy whispered as he threw his arms around Michael and hugged him. "You've been traveling a hard road, my dear friend."

"It's been interesting."

"Pearl," Paddy called, "he's here! Come along. He looks skinny as a winter-starved wolf, and I'll bet he can eat half a beef!"

"Not at the prices in this town."

"Don't worry about prices," Paddy said. Then, lowering his voice, "Don't tell Pearl, but I want you to put everything you spend in this town on my account. You just tell old Seth and whoever else you do business with that I'm paying the bill. Understand?"

"I can't do that," Michael protested. "It wouldn't be right."

"The hell it wouldn't. You and I are going to open another store in Sacramento and you're going to be the man in charge."

Michael blinked. "You can't be serious."

"Of course I am! But we can talk it over later. Pearl gets nervous when I talk business at the table. So let's have a few drinks, some laughs, and fatten you up, Mike!"

Paddy slapped him so hard on the back that Michael was knocked a couple of steps forward. In the old days he'd have banged him right back, only now it didn't seem right.

"Sure," Michael said. "Later."

"All ready," Pearl said, slipping between them and taking both their arms. "I sure do feel proud to be escorted by two such handsome and successful young Irishmen. I swear, Michael, you're going to set the young women's hearts to fluttering in Hangtown."

"I don't think so," he said, "and anyway I keep my mind and heart with Miss Tessa. Always will, too."

Paddy and Pearl, chubby, red-cheeked and as well matched as a pair of carriage ponies, exchanged serious glances, but they did not say anything, and that somehow struck Michael as being a little odd.

THE DINNER WAS THE BEST Michael had ever eaten. Paddy had ordered a delicious oyster stew, followed by halibut steaks and lobster tails on ice. For dessert they'd had chocolate mousse, and it went just fine with the second bottle of French wine.

Michael dared not think what that meal must have cost Paddy and Pearl, but they hadn't seemed the least bit concerned, so he'd dug right into his food and thoroughly enjoyed himself.

Now, when they were halfway through the second bottle of wine, Paddy again raised the question of Michael's future. "Mike," he said, "you couldn't have come at a better time."

"I suppose not," Michael said, still uncertain about Paddy's intentions.

Paddy selected a Cuban cigar from a tray carried by their waiter. "Want one, Mike?"

"No, thanks."

"You sure? They're the best that money can buy."

"I never smoke," Michael said, with a slight edge to his voice because he was starting to feel crowded. "You know that."

"Yeah, sure." Paddy lit his cigar. "In Sacramento I spoke before the legislature about this Foreign Miner's Tax business. I told them that it ought to be repealed."

"Good for you!" Michael said, pleased at this bit of news.

"Hell, yes! Now that the diggin's are getting played out, it's the Chinamen and Mexicans that'll keep prospecting, not the white people. We need to keep the dust flowing into our businesses. The Foreign Miner's Tax is driving the Mexicans and Orientals away. I don't like 'em any better than the next fella, but they'll work for every last speck of gold."

Michael opened his mouth to say something, thought better of it, then closed his mouth again and took another gulp of wine as Paddy continued.

"I think they'll repeal that tax, maybe as early as this summer. But, like I said, the Sierra streams can't last forever and that means that California's real future is in agriculture."

"Agriculture?"

"Sure! Agriculture and business. That's where the money is to be made. And since we aren't farmers, Mike, we take care of the business end of things. Understand?"

Michael made himself nod. He didn't like being lectured and he didn't like being called "Mike." Paddy knew that. However, Michael decided this was not a good time to correct Paddy. Not in front of his wife, and when he was paying for such a fine meal. But tomorrow he'd let Paddy know that his name was Michael, not Mike.

"So," Paddy was saying, "we find us a good Sacramento store location, buy in greater volume and earn greater per unit profits. That way, when the gold peters out here, we can concentrate on building even more volume of business in Sacramento. How's that sound? Makes good sense, doesn't it?"

Pearl said, "My father said you have a real head for business on your shoulders, Paddy. That's what he said right from the start."

Paddy beamed at the compliment and puffed up like a courting pigeon. Michael took another drink.

"Listen," he said, reaching into his coat pocket and drawing out the letter he'd written in the Mexican camp, "I would like to post this to Miss Tessa."

"I can do that tomorrow, first thing," Paddy said, reaching for the letter.

But Michael shook his head. "I'd rather do it myself. What I was wondering was, would you mind my using your store as a return address? You see, I've been in the gold fields since we parted and you know that there's no way I can stay in one camp. But if Miss Tessa could write to me in care of your store, I could hear from her again."

Paddy deflated a little. "Mike," he said, "you remember how angry you got the last time we discussed Miss Glynn?"

"I'm sorry about that."

"Don't be," Paddy said, waving his cigar. "It's just that I don't want her to come between us again. I'd just rather not have any part in this."

"But all I'm asking is to use your address so that I can hear from her!" Michael said, raising his voice. "Paddy, come on! I'm not asking for much. Just hold onto Tessa's letters when they arrive from New York."

"Paddy," Pearl said, growing anxious, "what harm could it do?"

Paddy emptied his wineglass. He would not look at Michael. "All right," he said, speaking to his empty plate. "But on one condition."

"What?" Michael asked, trying to keep from getting angry.

"I just don't want to ever fight about Miss Glynn with you again. Is that clear?"

"Sure."

"Okay, then," Paddy said, looking up and taking a deep

breath. "But after we get you that Sacramento store, Miss Glynn can send her letters there, right?"

It was Michael's turn to look down at the table for a moment. "Paddy," he said, "it won't work."

"What won't work?"

"Me in a general store. I'm just not cut out for it."

"How do you know that?"

"Paddy, please!" Pearl said anxiously. "Don't push him."

But Paddy was very upset. "Look around you, Mike! Do you see any prospectors in this room? Anyone that even has any calluses on his hands?"

Michael didn't have to look. He'd already judged the caliber of patrons and they all appeared to be prosperous business types.

"No."

"And you won't. Not tonight, not ever. The money is to be made in business and agriculture. I told you that. I want us to be rich, just like we talked about all those terrible months on the *Orion.* And we can do it! But only if you listen to my advice and follow it."

Paddy waved to the waiter. "Brandy, three glasses . . . and . . . oh, hell, bring the bottle."

"Paddy!" Pearl cried. "Don't drink too much. You're a councilman now. Everyone will be talking if you drink too much and get angry."

"I'm not going to get drunk."

"I might," Michael said.

"That's fine," Paddy said, "but not me."

When the brandy arrived with the three snifters, Paddy filled them to the brim and pinned Michael with his eyes. "To our joint success in Sacramento?"

He and Pearl raised their glasses and Michael just didn't have it in him not to do the same. "To Sacramento," he said without enthusiasm.

Their crystal glasses tinkled like little bells and they drank and everyone forced a smile.

"It's gonna be good for us," Paddy vowed. "Mike, you've

suffered too long. From now on, we're going first class for the rest of our lives!"

Michael believed him. He really did. But that being the case, why wasn't he excited and happy inside?

Seven

October 14, 1852

My Beloved Miss Tessa:

I have written you letters every other day since arriving in Hangtown and anxiously await to receive your sweet reply. *Please* write the first moment possible. We have so much to say to each other.

As I have been telling you, I do not much like the mercantile business and am poor at it, but Paddy hasn't given up on me and I am on a good salary. To save money, I am sleeping in the storeroom of our new Sacramento establishment. I have also found pasture for Nugget, who I ride every Sunday to preserve my sanity and restore my flagging spirits.

Despite my poor business sense, our mercantile is growing very fast. I am up to my ears in new supplies that arrive weekly by steamer from as far away as New York. How I wish by some magic I could open a packing crate and discover you reposing inside, waiting for me. I have more and more taken to fantasies like that about you.

Sacramento is booming because it is the jumping-off place for all the gold fields and the natural terminus of the Overland Trail where thousands of new immigrants arrive between May and November before the Sierra passes are clogged with snow.

I hope you are not disappointed that I still have not struck it rich. I know that I promised much more than the life of a storekeeper, but California is a very beautiful place and the weather, except when it is foggy, is beyond compare. Everything grows in our rich Central Valley soil and the fruit and vegetables are a wonder to taste and behold. I wish you could come to visit. Maybe you would like Sacramento and, if you did, I could be happy working in a mercantile just knowing that we would be comfortably fixed and always together in love and marriage.

Please write soon, Tessa. I have not heard from you since last we parted on the wharf exactly two long years ago. It seems like a lifetime, but I remain,

> Your devoted fiancé,
> MICHAEL W. CALLAHAN, Esq.

MICHAEL FOLDED THE LETTER, sealed and addressed the envelope, then laid a silver dollar beside it for the messenger who would arrive to carry it to the mail packet that steamed down to San Francisco every afternoon. He had eaten his meal quickly while writing his letter and now it was time to return to business.

This store was bigger than the one in Hangtown and Paddy had designed it so that the manager and his assistant could peer down most of the aisles and watch for customers who might need help finding something or take a notion to commit thievery. The aisles were almost always filled with men, many of them fresh off oceangoing vessels such as the *Orion*.

"Say, mister," a young man called, "how much is this here shovel?"

"Twenty-five dollars," Michael replied.

"Twenty-five dollars! Why, mister, you sure don't mean to get rich off just me, do ya?" the man asked, replacing the Ames shovel in its rack beside the picks and heavy iron pry bars.

Michael grinned sheepishly. "I know the prices are high, but they're even higher up in the gold fields."

"Well, how much are these big gold pans?" the would-be prospector asked, taking one in his hands and turning it this way and that.

"Ten dollars."

"Only got eight."

Michael hesitated. His assistant was standing close by and listening. "I'm sorry," Michael said, "but we'll have to have ten dollars."

The young man replaced the merchandise and shook his head hopelessly. "I come around Cape Horn and someone stole my pack the minute I arrived in San Francisco. Ain't got much of anything left, including money."

It was a story that Michael heard every day and he had a stock reply. "Want some advice?"

"Yes, sir," the young Argonaut said. "As long as it's free."

"Buy a good cast-iron frying pan and you can use it to pan gold until you get enough dust to buy a real prospector's pan. And by then, you might just want to use a long tom."

"I heard about those," the man said. "I heard they can help a man work five times the dirt more than he can pan."

"At least."

"You got any for sale?"

"Sure, but you can make your own far cheaper. Here," Michael said, pulling out a little paper sack and drawing a diagram. "I'll put in the dimensions and sell you a pound of nails. You can always borrow a hammer and saw in the camps, and although it might take you half a day to build one of these, it'll be time well spent."

The young man was staring at him. "How much you want for this diagram and the nails?"

The boy reminded Michael quite a lot of himself two years and what seemed like a lifetime ago. "How about a dollar?"

"A dollar? Why, that won't buy more than an apple or an egg in California."

"Maybe, but it'll also buy you a pound of nails on special right here and now," Michael said with a wink.

"Well, sir, thank you very much!"

Michael finished his drawing and scooped up a sack of nails without bothering to weigh them. "Here you go."

The young man paid, with a smile. "Any suggestion on whether I should go to the northern or the southern gold fields?"

"One is as good as the other," Michael said. "I worked the Stanislaus and had some luck. Might still be a good bet. I know the southern camps and they're still producing, although more and more gold is being found in dry diggin's."

The young Argonaut had hung on every word. "Then it's the southern mines I'm bound for. And say, you're a real fine fella. I'll remember you when I come back through here again, and when I got me a fat poke full of gold dust, I'll spend my share here."

"I'm counting on it," Michael called as the man took the diagram and nails, then departed.

"Mr. Callahan?"

Michael turned to his assistant. Alfred Willis was about his own age, serious, tight-fisted and good with figures. Alfred held Michael in contempt. The feeling was entirely mutual. Alfred had been ten years in the business and it grated him badly to have to work under a man who knew nothing about retailing and was constantly losing sales and profits.

"I beg your pardon, sir, but that was no way to run a business. You gave that man nearly *three* dollars' worth of nails, not one."

Michael feigned surprise. "Oh, really?"

"Yes . . . really. And Mr. Ryan won't be too happy about that."

"Then why don't we not tell him?"

Alfred raised his nose like a mongrel sniffing wind, then marched down an aisle. Michael couldn't abide the weasel-faced little skinflint and had an overpowering urge to grab him by the neck and throttle him. There was no doubt whatsoever that Alfred would tell Paddy about the pound of nails or that Paddy was going to be miffed.

To hell with it, Michael thought as he gazed out the front window and thought of Tessa, Rosita and then of Joaquín. It was funny how money changed the way that people affected your life. Take Paddy, for instance. Michael, though younger, had always been the leader. He'd been the one that had chased off the New York bullies with his fists. And when they'd been aboard the *Orion,* there'd been rough men who would have whipped Paddy and taken his few belongings, but Michael had whipped the leader of the bullies shortly after sailing out of New York Harbor and established for the remainder of the voyage that the strong would not take advantage of the weak. Once in California, Michael had made the decisions and worked the hardest in the rivers and streams. Now all that had changed and Paddy was the leader. Paddy Ryan made the important decisions. He was the man who set the prices, bought the shiploads of supplies and kept track of the accounts. Michael knew he was little more than an overpaid stock and sales clerk. A man could fool the public but he could not fool himself.

ON SUNDAY MORNING Michael rode Nugget along the Sacramento River, where cottonwood trees were ablaze with fall colors and the big paddle-wheel steamers thrashed the river into foam. Michael rode slowly, enjoying the fine day as he gave serious consideration to leaving Sacramento and returning to the gold fields in the hope of striking it rich. The truth was that his spirits were at rock bottom, even if his bank account and standing in the community were on the rise.

"What's wrong with me?" he asked Nugget. "I'm gaining weight, eating three good meals a day, sleeping on a real bed instead of the ground and people in this town are beginning to know my name. I should be happy as a tick on a fat dog, but I'm not. I hate being cooped up all day and I've no mind at all for prices. I want to save these hard-luck prospectors money, not wrestle as much as I can from them."

Nugget tossed his head and continued along the riverbank as Michael watched the boats. When one passed, Michael heard the strum of a Mexican guitar and he thought again of Joaquín. What was the vaquero up to now that the California legislature had just repealed the Greaser's Act and Foreign Miner's Tax? Had Joaquín and his people returned to Sonora? One thing Michael knew for sure—Joaquín Murieta was a vaquero and no more cut out for prospecting than he was for clerking in a store. Obviously it was one of life's unfairnesses that men usually had to work at whatever paid the most money, not what they loved or did well.

That afternoon Michael rode up the middle fork of the American River past crumbling Sutter's Fort and on into the cooler foothills, where he could smell the pines and listen to their soft whispers. He remained until sunset to watch liquid gold creep across the great Central Valley and then he rode slowly back down to Sacramento.

It was nearly ten o'clock when he finally returned to the mercantile and let himself in the front door. He started past the darkened counter toward the storeroom but froze when he heard the scrape of a chair.

"Who's there!"

Paddy Ryan dropped his feet to the floor with a loud thump. "It's me."

"Paddy!" Michael exclaimed with relief. "What the deuce are you doing sitting here in the dark at this hour?"

"Gettin' drunk, my friend."

Michael lit a candle and placed it on the counter. "What's wrong?"

"Have a drink."

Michael figured that he'd better have several drinks. Whatever was afoot was not going to be pleasant. He took a long pull on the whiskey. It was top-grade stuff, smooth and fiery. It made his eyes water.

"What is it, Paddy?"

"It's about you."

Michael took another drink. "I can guess. Alfred has been telling you about me and you've finally decided to let me go. That's it, isn't it?"

"No. I'd fire Alfred first."

"That'd be a mistake. He's got ten times my head for business."

Paddy stood up heavily and reached inside his coat to produce a letter. The moment Michael saw it, he felt a ball of ice form in his gut.

"It's from Tessa," Paddy said, roughly shoving the letter across the counter.

"Why'd you get it instead of me? Tessa knows to write to me here."

"Maybe you'd better read it yourself."

Michael started to reach for the letter, then jerked his hand back. He swallowed and could not tear his eyes from the long-awaited letter. "Why don't you just tell me what it says."

Paddy took another drink, a long one. Michael did the same. Paddy cleared his throat. "Tessa didn't have enough guts to tell you herself, so she's asked me to tell you."

"Tell me what?"

"She's been married a year now to a lawyer. They've even got a baby boy."

Michael froze and heard himself say, "I've got some bad news for you too, Paddy. I'm quittin' as of right now. I'm going back to the southern gold fields."

"Don't let Tessa ruin this too."

"She's got nothing to do with it," he whispered. "You see, I just went riding up into the pines and it came to me that I need to go back to the mountains. I miss them. I really . . . really do."

"Mike, listen to me!" Paddy pleaded. "Do you remember how thin and worn down you were when you arrived in Hangtown this spring? You didn't have twenty dollars to your name. Now, you've got respect, money and a chance to get rich. Don't throw that away. Not for Tessa, not for anything!"

But Michael wasn't listening. "The Mexicans down around Sonora call me the Gringo Amigo. Did I ever tell you that story?"

"No." Paddy drank savagely.

"Then I'll tell you while we get drunk together," Michael said, trying hard to recall every detail of his first meeting with the Mexicans on the Stanislaus, the day men had died.

Michael spent the next hour recounting how a bullet creased his cheek, the dying Mexican boy and how he had felt deep inside. Talking helped. It occupied his mind and gave him time to recover from the crushing disappointment of Tessa's letter.

"So that's why—to them—I'll always be the Gringo Amigo."

"Maybe we could open a big store together in Sonora," Paddy said finally. "They'd buy from you."

"No, thanks."

After a long silence, Paddy burped and said, "So, Mike, when you leaving?"

"In the morning."

Paddy drew out another cigar and lit it. "Stay warm, and if you need help you know where you can find it."

"Yeah."

"Will you at least keep in touch?"

"I will."

"Goddamn that girl!" Paddy cried. "Damn her to hell!"

Michael glanced sideways at Paddy and saw tears streaming down his friend's cheeks. "You're going to be rich and important here someday," Michael said. "Alfred will make it happen a whole lot faster."

Paddy tried to speak but choked and failed, so Michael just patted him on the shoulder and went to bed.

Eight

MICHAEL LEFT SACRAMENTO before dawn the next morning. He had not slept a wink since learning that Tessa had married. It occurred to Michael that he should have said good-bye to Paddy and thanked him for a chance to get back on his feet with some money in the bank, but it just wasn't in him.

Daylight found Michael riding down through the same gold towns that he'd passed through six months before, only now his spirits were so low that he had little interest in his surroundings. Even Nugget seemed depressed, and instead of prancing down the road, the sorrel gelding was content to lower its head and plod.

"It's back to the lean times," Michael told the animal. "No more fresh straw and warm stall. No more grain and currying every few days. From now on, it's just a matter of us surviving in the gold fields along with everyone else."

In reply, Nugget shook his head and snorted with seeming disgust.

When Michael reached Sonora, he saw a Mexican named Miguel Escobar and hailed the man in the street. Escobar was a shy fellow in his twenties and a great admirer of Joaquín Murieta.

"Where is Joaquín these days, señor?" Michael asked in Spanish.

"He and Rosita live in Agua Fria, Señor Gringo Amigo. They have a cabin a little to the east of town along a small stream."

"Gracias," Michael said as he started to ride past.

"Gringo Amigo?"

"Yes?"

"Why do you look so sad?"

"Because a woman has broken my heart," Michael confessed.

Miguel's eyes filled with pity. "It is the same with me, señor. Good women are bad for good men. No?"

"I'll have to think about that one sometime," Michael said as he continued on south.

He spent a week in the mining area around Mount Bullion, where the Princeton Mine was producing more than five thousand dollars of gold a day, infusing the southern gold fields with excitement, jobs and boomtown prosperity. Michael had to force himself to search for unmined areas of quartz, and when he found nothing promising, he gave up too easily and rode on toward Agua Fria, which meant "cold water" in Spanish.

Agua Fria was a little Sonora, with a large Mexican population working the nearby hills, rivers and streams. As far as Michael could tell, the town was barely subsisting and most of the town's white inhabitants had already moved to Mount Bullion for the jobs and a greater likelihood of making a strike.

When Michael rode into the little clapboard collection of shacks and vacant stores, he felt the hostility of many Mexicans who did not recognize him. They deeply resented all gringos because of the discrimination that they had suffered. The hated Foreign Miner's Tax, though repealed, still rankled the Mexican people and the bitterness was hidden just below the surface, ready to explode.

"Hey, Gringo!" a big Mexican yelled, stepping out from a saloon. "I like your horse. You want to sell him to me?"

"No," Michael said, "he's not for sale, señor."

"Maybe if I pull my pistol and shoot you in the belly, maybe then you will sell him to me, eh, Gringo?"

Michael was wearing his own gun, but he hadn't had much

time to practice firing it while in Sacramento and he sure didn't think he would be able to hit anything from horseback. He kept riding until the Mexican, reeking of tequila, rushed over and grabbed his horse by the bit.

"I said I want to buy this horse, señor. And I will give you a hundred pesos."

"And I said he is not for sale," Michael said quietly. "Now let go of him so that I can pass."

But the Mexican's dark features twisted with hatred. "Gringos are not welcome in Agua Fria."

"I am looking for Joaquín Murieta, who calls me the Gringo Amigo. Now I think you had better let go of my horse's bit or I'll climb down and beat on your drunken head. Comprende?"

The Mexican blinked with surprise, then confusion. "You are the Gringo Amigo?"

"I am."

The Mexican considered this piece of information, then arrived at a conclusion. "And *I* am Juan Torres. I still do not like you, señor."

"And I don't like you either, Juan. So let go of my horse and we will both be rid of each other."

Torres released Nugget's bit, but not before he jerked the horse's mouth painfully, causing it to throw its head and rear back on its haunches. Torres laughed because it was all Michael could do to keep from being unseated and dumped in the street as he clung off-balance, hugging Nugget's neck.

When Michael finally did regain his seat and composure, he was furious—furious enough to jump down from the animal, wind his reins around a hitching rail and come straight at Torres with balled fists.

The smile never left Torres' face as he raised his own fists, then swung his boot for Michael's knee. The boot grazed Michael's calf as his fist exploded against the Mexican's jaw, knocking him to the ground amid shouts of onlookers.

Torres was up in a hurry, rubbing his jaw and cursing.

"Come on," Michael goaded, "let's see what you can do with your fists instead of your mouth, Señor Torres!"

Torres outweighed Michael by a good forty pounds, but he was drunk and he was slow. His big arms moved a lot of air but damn little else as Michael drove a right uppercut into his soft belly, then a left cross to the side of his ear that dropped him again, cursing even louder.

"Get up," Michael ordered, shaking off his depression for the first time since learning of Tessa's marriage. "Get up and fight!"

Torres came storming to his feet, grabbing for his pistol. Michael went for his own gun but he knew he was going to be too late so he lunged forward in a desperate attempt to grab Torres' gun hand.

His fingers closed around Torres' right wrist and he smashed the wrist downward against his knee. The gun exploded, driving a bullet harmlessly into the dirt before Michael smashed the wrist down once more and the gun itself went flying.

Michael was not going to take any more chances. Torres was a bad man and he would probably have another gun hidden on him someplace, or at least a knife. Michael gave him the chance to use neither as his hard, bony fists drew blood and bruises each time they landed. When Torres cried out and dropped to the ground, Michael stepped back and lowered his hands.

He turned and headed for his horse but had not taken ten steps before he heard a cry of warning and then two shots so closely spaced they sounded almost like one. Michael threw himself at the ground, rolled, clawed for his own pistol, then froze to see Torres holding his stomach as blood seeped between his fingers. Torres' mouth opened and closed. His eyes rolled up toward his forehead and he pitched headfirst into the dirt.

Michael looked to the left, where a man stood holding a smoking pistol. "Reyes!"

Reyes Feliz holstered his pistol. He was a handsome young man, no more than twenty. Michael had met him once in Sonora. He was Rosita's brother and one of Joaquín's closest friends.

Normally smiling and happy, his expression was very grim and when he came to Michael's side he did not waste words.

"Come, Señor Callahan, we will go to visit Joaquín and my sister. Did you know that they are married now?"

Michael shook his head, tearing his eyes from Torres, who was now surrounded by townspeople standing helplessly, watching him labor for breath.

"We can't just leave him like that!"

"He will be dead before we are gone," Reyes said. "Besides, he has no amigos, that one."

Michael remounted his horse and was joined a moment later by Reyes. They galloped off to the east, Reyes turning only once to glance over his shoulder. Michael looked too. He saw the people walking away from Torres.

WHEN THEY APPROACHED THE CABIN high up on the mountainside, they saw Joaquín and Rosita working a long tom beside a mountain stream. The sight of Joaquín, dressed in baggy miner's pants with a work shirt and a slouch hat on his head did nothing to raise Michael's spirits.

"It does not seem right that a vaquero like Joaquín should do that kind of work."

"It is honest work," Reyes said, "but it has no dignity. Joaquín does not talk about it much."

"Are they panning any color?"

"Sí. But they are not getting rich."

"Not many are," Michael said, then amended himself as he thought of Paddy, adding, "except the merchants."

When Joaquín recognized them, he dropped his shovel, threw his hat away as if it embarrassed him, then approached them with a big smile.

"Gringo Amigo!" he cried. "It is good to see you again! Where is your woman?"

Michael dismounted. "She married another man."

Joaquín's smile faded, but only for a moment. "If I had known that, you could have married Rosita! She would have chosen you over me, señor!"

Rosita laughed. In a simple white peasant dress and sandals, she was prettier than Michael had ever seen her before. "The outdoors becomes you, señora," Michael said. "You look very lovely today."

Rosita actually blushed, causing both her husband and her brother to laugh heartily.

"Come," Joaquín said, "we will have a celebration!"

"With what, my husband?" Rosita asked. "We have no gold and very little food."

The smiles died. Michael grabbed an extra shovel and threw a scoop into the long tom. "Then we will just have to work hard for our supper tonight," he said, suddenly liking the prospect of a good four or five hours of hard work.

Reyes was not quite so enthusiastic about the idea but he made a good show of working the long tom with Rosita while Joaquín and Michael shoveled.

All afternoon they toiled steadily and their hard work had very little reward—less than one ounce of dust gained by evening.

"It is enough for a bottle of tequila, some flour for tortillas and maybe some beef and corn."

"Not beef," Rosita said. "Tortillas, corn and tequila only."

Joaquín shrugged. Michael had been watching him work and he could see that the vaquero was thinner than he'd been. His quick smile could not hide the fact that life as a prospector was grinding him down. As much as Michael hated to admit it, he thought that in two, maybe three years the vaquero's spirit would be broken. All that would remain of Joaquín would be the trappings of his once proud trade, the spurs, the rawhide reata, the Spanish bit and the festive outfit that he wore on Sundays, the one with the silver coins sewn in the outside seams of his trousers.

Late that evening, after their simple dinner and while sipping slowly on the last of their tequila, they reposed on the porch and talked of many things. Michael told them about the letter and they listened without comment until Joaquín could contain his anger no longer and called Tessa something that could not be repeated.

"It is done," Michael said. "Paddy tried to warn me right from the start, but I wouldn't listen."

"Why did you leave her in New York, señor?" Reyes asked.

"I was poor Irish. Tessa was middle-class Irish and she and her family wanted the best. If I'd struck it rich in these gold fields right away, like I'd planned and promised, I'd have won her hand. But I failed."

"No," Rosita said firmly. *"She* failed. Her heart was not true and she did not deserve your love."

"That is so," Reyes said, his head thrown back and his eyes fixed on the heavens. "A woman who does not wait for a man is not worth so much heartache, Señor Callahan. Maybe you are better off without her."

Michael couldn't answer that one. As far as he was concerned, Tessa Glynn was the most beautiful young woman in the world and, though her love had not proved strong, he had failed to keep his promise. Michael had left her more than two years earlier and still hadn't a damn thing to show for it except a fine horse and saddle that had been a gift, and a thousand dollars or so that he'd deposited in a Sacramento bank account.

"I should never have taken your gold and claim after you were almost killed by those three coyotes," Joaquín lamented. "If you had kept that gold, you might have won her heart."

"I spit on her heart!" Rosita said angrily, spitting once or twice into the dirt to emphasize her point.

Joaquín threw an arm around his lovely wife. "You spit on nothing," he said, with a smile of amusement.

Rosita started to argue, but when she looked into her husband's eyes the argument died on her lips and she kissed him passionately instead.

Michael glanced quickly away. He was happy for Joaquín and Rosita because it was obvious that they were very much in love despite their hard circumstances. Out in front of the cabin was a meadow, and Nugget was now hobbled and grazing beside Joaquín's horse as well as that of Reyes. There was no money for hay. Michael wondered if his friends would even be able to keep their fine horses through the winter. The idea of vaqueros like Reyes and Joaquín being reduced to such a hard and undignified existence was very depressing.

"Joaquín," Michael said, "tomorrow I will go looking for some quartz."

Joaquín laughed in a nice, easy way. "I am afraid, senor, that many others have learned your trick. There is no more new quartz. It has all been found."

"I don't believe that," Michael said after a moment. "I think I can find more. It might take a long time, but time is all I have now."

Joaquín considered this as he sipped on the bottle, then passed it to Reyes, who took a short pull, then handed it to Rosita, who shook her head.

"Amigo," Joaquín said, "maybe first, before you go hunting for quartz, you need to find a *good* woman."

"No, thanks," Michael said quickly. "I've had enough of women for a while."

"Maybe, maybe not," Joaquín said. "But tomorrow I have need of things in Hornitos and we will go there."

Joaquín winked at his young brother-in-law. "I would take you too, Reyes, but you are too young and too innocent."

Reyes laughed out loud, and so did his sister who said, "Reyes with the baby face. The women love my little brother so much he puts *them* all to bed at night!"

Michael joined the laughter, but his mind was dead set against finally going to meet Aurora López in Hornitos. He would make that plain in the morning. It was not worth being stubborn about tonight when everyone was having so much fun. In fact, it surprised Michael that he could laugh again at all. When he had ridden out of Sacramento, leaving Paddy and his hopes behind, he had thought that laughter was something that would never be possible again.

The next morning Michael awoke very early, as was his custom. Joaquín, Rosita and even young Reyes awakened early too.

"I can't go to Hornitos with you," Michael argued. "Besides, we need to find more gold, not another woman."

Rosita laughed. "Maybe we do need another woman with us! Someone to help me cook and take care of things when I am not working beside my husband in the stream, no?"

"Reyes," Joaquín said, "you must stay here with Rosita until we return."

"Sí."

Michael heard the concern in their voices. "What's wrong?"

"Por nada."

"Don't give me that," Michael said with irritation. "Is something wrong?"

The two vaqueros shrugged, but under Michael's steady gaze Reyes said, "There have been attacks against our people by . . . by the gringos."

"But why? The tax has been repealed. What is it now?"

"It is the same thing it has always been, Amigo. One people against another people."

"I don't see what anyone could want up on this mountainside," Michael said. "I doubt that even the Chinese would give it so much as a second glance."

"This is true," Joaquín said, "and that is why there is nothing to worry about. It is just not good for a beautiful woman to be left alone in the mountains. Comprende?"

"Sí," Michael said.

"Then we go now."

Michael saw that there was no use in arguing. Joaquín was bound and determined to take him to meet Aurora López and do whatever business he had to do in Hornitos. Anyway, Michael did need supplies before he could go quartz hunting in the higher mountains. The days were getting shorter and the leaves were already starting to edge copper and gold. Up higher in the mountains, the leaves would be ablaze with color.

"Then let's ride, señor," Michael said, impatient to be gone and return.

Joaquín laughed and, as if he could read his mind, said, "Once you see her, Amigo, you might not be in such a hurry to return. You might even want to spend the cold winter in Hornitos, eh, Amigo?"

Joaquín and Reyes laughed, but Michael was in no mood for ribald humor. He had a headache from the cheap tequila, and he discovered that he was suddenly anxious to return and find more gold. Not for Tessa Glynn, but for himself and Joaquín, Rosita and even for Reyes, who had saved his life.

A man needed a purpose. Finding quartz and then gold was about the only good reason Michael had to exist now that Tessa was gone. If a man couldn't have love, perhaps money was the next best thing.

Nine

AS THEY RODE down the western Sierra slopes toward the great Central Valley and Hornitos, Joaquín was in an especially talkative mood. He explained that Hornitos, like Agua Fria, was mostly inhabited by Mexicans, many of whom had been driven off their claims at Quartzburg and Mount Bullion.

"Hornitos, Amigo, means 'little ovens' in Spanish."

"Little ovens?"

"Sí," Joaquín said, "it is a name given because of the tombs you will see on the hillsides below the chapel. No one knows who was buried there long ago, but they were Mexicans and their tombs are shaped like square bake ovens."

"I see."

Joaquín frowned and shook his head sadly. "Two years ago a terrible thing happened in Hornitos. A Chinaman was torn apart."

Michael stared. "Torn apart?"

"Sí. His name was Ling and he was a good friend of the Mexican people. A gringo would not leave him alone and finally Ling shot the man. He was thrown in jail and the gringos tried to break into jail, but it was too strong because, as you will see, it is made of rock and we would not let them in through the front door."

Joaquín rolled a cigarette and lit it before he continued. "So the gringos sneaked around behind the jail. One crept under the barred window and held up a fresh plug of tobacco. When Ling reached for it through the bars, they grabbed Ling's wrists. Next, they tied a reata around them and spurred their horses away, tearing the poor Chinaman apart."

Michael shuddered. "I'm afraid that the gringos dislike the Chinese even more than your people, Joaquín."

The vaquero waved his hand with an apparent show of indifference. "Except for Ling, I do not like Orientals either. But it was a bad way for a man to die. I think it put a curse on the town."

"Does Aurora live there?"

Joaquín chuckled. "So, you *are* thinking of her! That is good, Amigo. And many times I have told her about you."

"Why?" Michael asked with asperity. "You know that I had always been in love with another."

Joaquín, always ready with a quick answer or a quick laugh, was uncharacteristically silent for a good long while before he said, "I think somehow that Señorita López and yourself would find each other's company, how you say it . . . ah, very simpatico."

The tips of the vaquero's drooping mustache twitched. "You see, the señorita also keeps a diary."

Michael almost laughed out loud. "Is *that* it? The fact that we both keep diaries?"

Joaquín assumed an injured expression. "It is important, no? Does it not say something about how you think and feel?"

"Well, yes, but many people keep diaries, and they may have absolutely nothing in common except that they enjoy putting their thoughts and impressions down on paper."

"Then they should read each other's diaries and maybe they would fall in love," Joaquín said with great patience, as if this ought to be very obvious.

Michael looked away, knowing that it was useless to argue with the vaquero. You could not logically argue matters of the heart with an incurable romantic. To Michael's way of thinking, this entire conversation was ridiculous.

"There is something else," Joaquín said after they had ridden another mile.

Michael waited in silence. Joaquín asked, "Don't you want to know?"

"Yes."

"Like you, Señorita López also had her heart broken."

Michael's expression softened. "I'm sorry. Did she tell you this?"

"She did not have to, Amigo, because *I* am the one that broke her heart when I met Rosita."

"You're amazing, Joaquín. By introducing us, are you trying to ease your conscience?"

"I have no conscience," Joaquín said. "But Señorita López is a very beautiful woman. And she, like myself, comes from the royal Castilian blood of Spain. From the conquistadores! And before Mexico stole the ranchos from the Spanish grandees thirty years ago, Señor Luis Antonio López owned many thousands of cattle, horses and sheep. My father once worked for Señor López as a vaquero and he told me of the great fiestas on the special days of the saints."

"I have heard that the vaqueros once roped grizzlies in the foothills for sport and dragged them to the arenas to fight the wild Spanish bulls. Is this true?"

"It is," Joaquín said, with a faraway look in his eyes. "When my father was a young vaquero, he said that the great 'oso pardo,' the 'grizzly bear,' would often come down from the mountains and ridges to attack Don López' herds of cattle. The first time my father saw vaqueros go after the grizzly on horseback, he remembered that they would grease the first thirty feet of their reatas back from the hondo."

"Grease their reatas?"

"Sí. Otherwise, the bear would be able to grab the reata and pull a horse into its jaws."

"I see." Michael clucked his tongue with wonder. "I cannot imagine what skill it must have taken."

"And what courage!" Joaquín exclaimed. "They would have to rope the bear several times from different directions so that it could not overtake and knock down a horse and rider. And then they would either kill the bear or drag it to the plaza arenas to fight the great black Spanish bulls."

"Who would win?"

"The bear," Joaquín said without a moment's hesitation. "Unless it was weak or old—or the bull got lucky."

"What would they do with the bear when it had killed the bull?"

"Bring in more bulls until the bear was gored to death."

"So it could never win."

"No, Amigo. It is like with the Mexicans in California. Even if we fight and win the first battle, we must finally lose. So, if a Mexican fights, he must always remember that he will one day be shot or hanged by the gringos. To be shot is not so bad, I think, but to die strangling on the end of a rope—this I would never allow. Much better to die fighting, eh?"

Michael thought about that for a while as they approached Hornitos. "Do you ever think of living in peace down in Mexico?"

"No," Joaquín said. "This country is where I was born. It is in my bones."

"But maybe in Mexico things would be better."

"This," Joaquín repeated, "is my home. I will stay, and if I must die, let it be in a good fight, with dignity."

Michael said nothing more as they rode slowly into town. Hornitos appeared as sleepy as the Mexican settlement of Agua Fria and Michael felt the same hostility directed toward him with his sandy-colored hair and blue eyes.

Several hard-faced Mexicans were drinking beer in front of a cantina and Michael was sure that one of them would have stepped out into the street and challenged him if he had not been in the company of Joaquín.

The vaquero seemed to know everyone. He was flattered by two pretty girls who came rushing out from another cantina, laughing and tossing their heads to show off their shiny dark hair. They conversed in such rapid Spanish that Michael could not understand their words, but he did hear the name Señorita López and he saw the young girls look at him a little strangely when Joaquín told them he was the Gringo Amigo.

"What was all that about?" Michael asked as they rode on.

"It was nothing. I only told them that you were the Gringo Amigo and that if Aurora did not please you, then I would bring you back to dance and make love with them both."

"You didn't!"

Joaquín's black eyes flashed mirth. "I did not want you to be without good company tonight."

"*I'll* decide whose company I want, not you!"

"Not in Hornitos," Joaquín said. "But come, let us not fight. We are on our way to see the beautiful señorita and her poor father. It is not good to arrive at a guest's house with anger in your heart."

Michael supposed that Joaquín was right, so no more was said of the cantina girls. An hour later, they topped a low ridge and beheld a stream running through a long, green valley some three or four miles wide and at least ten miles long. The grass was tall and golden in late summer but interwoven with dark green ribbons of marsh grass fed by meandering streams. The entire valley was punctuated by clusters of huge California oak with their gnarled bark and their massive and highly unusual configurations of twisting gray branches.

In the distance, Michael could see the outline of what once had been a great hacienda. But even from a long way off, the adobe buildings appeared to be crumbling and several of their roofs were collapsed.

"It was Rancho San Pablo in the days of the Spanish dons and the Californios. This whole valley belonged to Don Luis López."

"But no longer?"

"No," Joaquín said. "The land was taken by the Mexican government before we were born and then the Mexicans lost it to the Americanos. Only through the kindness of a good man is Don Luis allowed to remain on the land until his death. That will be soon, Amigo. And then the beautiful señorita will be driven away, homeless, like a peasant."

"What will she do then?"

"I don't know. Maybe find a husband, maybe find a priest. Who is to say?"

Joaquín touched his big spur rowels to the flanks of his gray stallion and set it into an easy gallop that Michael had no difficulty matching. They rode stirrup to stirrup across the grassy valley with the sun warming their faces and clouds of grasshoppers swarming up in their wake. Michael was interested most in the old hacienda, but he could not help glancing sideways at Joaquín.

The vaquero rode ramrod straight, and although his body appeared rigid, up close Michael could see that it was not. Joaquín was completely relaxed. A faint smile played at the corners of his mouth and he had never looked happier. Michael could not help feeling good too. Despite the ache in his heart, the strength of his horse and the beauty of the day lifted his spirits. He was proud to ride side by side with Joaquín.

A quarter mile from the old ranch, they brought their fine horses to a walk. This provided Michael with a better chance to study the crumbling adobe hacienda and rickety pole corral containing two horses, and a black and white milk cow whose curving horns joined over her head like the woven handle of a wicker basket. Chickens and goats mingled in the yard. An old, mange-ravaged dog crawled stiffly to its feet and wobbled forward, hairless tail wagging in a half-hearted greeting.

It was apparent that the rancho had once been impressive but now had fallen on very hard times. Even the windows were covered with stiff cowhides instead of filled with glass panes, and leather hinges supported the door. Somewhere inside the hacienda a baby was crying fitfully, and two cats slept on the wide windowsills.

When they came to a hitch rail, Michael started to dismount, but Joaquín said, "No, Amigo. We must first be invited to step down by Don Luis or the señorita."

Michael, who had been lifting his left leg over his cantle, dropped it back across his horse and jammed his boot in the stirrup. "You must excuse me. I have no sense of the manners of these people. Poor Irish don't hold much with manners where I was raised."

Joaquín was about to say something when the heavy wooden door and a small, very old Mexican appeared. He was wearing black pants, white shirt and a burgundy-colored vest with fancy stitching. His head was bare and he was white-maned and bearded. In his thin brown hand was a cane with a silver handle and tip.

When Joaquín removed his hat, Michael did the same. "Don Luis, it is good to see you once again," Joaquín said, very formally.

The old don nodded so imperceptibly that Michael wasn't sure he had even seen the man's prominent chin dip. Don Luis reminded Michael of a hardwood stick, brittle but not easily broken. "Señor Murieta," Don Luis said without the warmth Michael had expected, "welcome."

"I come with a friend."

"A gringo?" The old don's shaggy white eyebrows rose in question.

"He is called among our people the Gringo Amigo," Joaquín explained. "He saved Mexican lives and was almost killed for his trouble. He is very brave and has a good heart. I have come to introduce him to you and your beautiful daughter."

The old man appeared neither impressed nor pleased and Michael swallowed nervously. "Don Luis," he blurted, "if this is inconvenient, I will go now."

The old man studied him for a moment, then stiffly turned and beckoned into the hacienda. A moment later, Señorita Aurora López appeared.

At first impression, the woman was not nearly as lovely as

Tessa or Rosita. But when Aurora smiled, her large brown eyes shamed the California sun and Michael gaped like a fool. She was tall, her features were strong and if he had to describe her in a word it would have been "regal." Dressed in a simple black skirt and white blouse with lace cuffs and lace collar folding down like the petals of a white rose under her chin, Aurora Lopéz conveyed great dignity and also great passion.

"Señor Callahan," she said, her eyes frank and a little questioning, "I have heard much of you and your writing. I look forward to discussing great literary works. We have a fine library and I'm sure that you have read and studied all the classics."

"No, señorita," Michael confessed, "I have not."

A hint of disappointment crossed her eyes, or so Michael thought. It was so fleeting he could not be sure, and her smile remained so radiant that Michael was emboldened to hastily add, "But I do like to read and would treasure your thoughts on any literary subject, Señorita López."

This seemed to please her, and Michael had the impression he might have redeemed himself a little. A few moments later, an old vaquero with a bad limp took the reins of their sweaty horses and led them away as Michael and Joaquín were ushered inside.

The interior of the hacienda was cool and dim. It took several moments for Michael's eyes to adjust to the poor light. When they did, he saw a room filled with dark, heavy furniture, cowhide rugs and, over a rock fireplace, the head of one great brindled steer with at least a twelve-foot-long span of black-tipped horns. A silver-mounted saddle held a place of honor near the western wall, and there were lush plants hanging in clay pots near the windows, something that Michael had never seen in a home, and only in a few of the best shops in New York City.

A moment later a young Mexican with a baby in her arms appeared with refreshments—tortillas, pieces of spicy beef, and the inevitable peppers which Michael avoided. A cool drink was pressed into his hands as they were seated on massive chairs and couches covered with cowhide.

The conversation was in Spanish, and spoken so rapidly that

Michael struggled to understand. It wasn't until the old don asked him a question that English was spoken for his benefit.

Señorita López said nothing at all as she sat primly beside her father, who reminisced about the old days and the skill of the vaquero.

"Do you know how to judge the roping skill of a vaquero?" Don Luis asked.

"No," Michael said, because the question was directed to him and not to Joaquín, who would undoubtedly know the expected answer.

Don Luis was delighted to educate his guest. "A true vaquero, in my time, could be mounted on his horse standing flat-footed and rope a bull as it was driven past him at a hard run. Then, before the bull hit the end of the reata, he could pull up his slack, take two quick turns around his saddle horn and, when the bull hit the end of the reata, loosen the slack so gently that the bull was brought to a standstill without hurting itself or jerking his horse off its feet."

Don Luis smiled broadly. Joaquín and Aurora did the same, but Michael, not fully appreciating the extreme difficulty involved, simply shook his head. "That must have been tough, huh?"

The smile on the old don's face faded. " 'Tough,' señor? It took years of practice, and even then, many could never equal this feat."

"Well," Michael said, "I'm no roper. Never even tried to rope, but I've seen my friend Joaquín gallop through a village roping dogs, chickens, cats and about anything else with a neck and shoulders. I'll tell you, he's a genius with a reata."

Joaquín visibly winced at this supposed compliment.

"You rope *chickens, cats* and *dogs?*" Don Luis asked, turning to address Joaquín with a mixture of disgust and disbelief.

Joaquín shifted uncomfortably. "Sometimes," he admitted. "But just to keep in practice."

Don Luis was visibly offended that a vaquero would stoop so low, and when Joaquín shot Michael a look of pure murder, it was obvious enough to him that he was to keep his mouth shut about such things in the future.

"Maybe, Señorita Aurora," Joaquín said, "you could show my amigo that pretty little filly I mean to break for you someday."

Aurora, with a smile of amusement, nodded. "Perhaps you would like to see her, señor?"

"Sure!" Michael said too eagerly.

They passed through a long hallway and outside into a huge courtyard filled with flowers and half-covered by an old grape arbor. The patio floor was laid with red-stained adobe bricks so carefully fitted together that a man would have had difficulty slipping even the blade of a knife between them. The west end of the courtyard was dominated by a life-sized marble statue of a saint holding a hand-carved oak bowl and crucifix.

"This courtyard is beautiful."

"I spend much time here with my father," Aurora said. "In the old days, when we had the fiestas, this would be a place of music and laughter. My father tells me that the fiestas might last ten days and that the music, dancing, singing and feasting would never stop."

"But this was before your time."

"Sí. My mother died when I was very small, and by then the government of Mexico had taken my father's land and given it to others. I have never seen this courtyard filled with happy people. Only my father and I, talking of days long gone that I never knew and that he cannot leave."

The young woman spoke with such sadness that Michael was deeply moved. "You cannot always live in the past, señorita. You are young and must live in your own time, not the time of your father."

"I have, Señor Callahan, lived some in my own time. I have lived and . . . yes, even loved."

When she said that, her chin lifted and her eyes were almost defiant. Michael looked away for a moment. "I am glad," he said, "for I have loved too and lost."

"I know. Joaquín told me. He tells me everything."

"How much do you know about *his* past?" Michael asked, wanting to divert the conversation away from himself.

"He was born in Alamos, a small village in Sonora, Mexico. His mother was said to be a descendant of the Rubios of Cadiz, Spain, and his father was Mayo."

"An Indian?"

"Yes. I realized this the very first time I looked into Joaquín's eyes. The Mayo are a light-skinned tribe that live in the Sonoran highlands. Joaquín's father worked in the silver mines but died in an accident when he was very young."

"When did Joaquín leave Mexico?"

"At the age of thirteen. He came north on foot where he worked for the Mexican ranchers and learned to be a vaquero. For several years before the gold rush he made his living catching wild horses."

"I see."

Aurora was smiling secretly to herself, and this caused Michael to raise his eyebrows in question. "What is it you are not telling me?"

"It is about the first time that we kissed. I do not think that you would want to hear the story."

She was right, but pride prevented Michael from admitting the fact. "Yes, I would."

"All right, then," Aurora said, her eyes bright and shining. "We were in this very courtyard, sitting on that stone bench under the climbing rose when he told me about a custom he remembered as a small boy."

Michael waited with little interest.

"In Alamos, and perhaps in all villages of Mexico, there is a custom among the boys and girls. On a special feast day in spring, the boys pick beautiful flowers and meet the girls in the plaza. With the whole village watching, the boys begin to walk clockwise around the plaza. The girls also walk, but counter-clockwise."

Aurora smiled happily. "When a boy meets the girl of his

dreams, he offers her flowers, and these she *cannot* refuse as she continues around the plaza."

"But . . ."

Michael's protest died as Aurora continued. "She cannot refuse, and if the girl likes the boy who gave her the flowers, she keeps them. But if not, the next time they come around to meet in the circle, she thanks the young boy very much and returns his flowers. In this kind and gracious way, the matter is closed and the boy will never lose his heart to her again."

"It's nice," Michael said, touched by the gentle simplicity of the custom and the delight that Aurora took in retelling it. "I wish that American girls had such a compassionate way of telling the boys who love them that they are not interested."

"I know," Aurora said, her eyes distant as she looked back in time. "After Joaquín told me this custom of his village, he picked a rose for me and one for himself. And then we walked around this courtyard and he gave me his flower and I kept it. He kissed me then . . . and I still have the flower pressed between the pages of a book."

Michael could see that Aurora's eyes had begun to shine with tears. Impulsively he reached out and touched her cheek. "Can we see that filly now?"

Aurora nodded and slipped her hand through his arm. "I think that would be a very fine idea, señor. But then, I want to talk to you about writing in diaries. I have never believed that a man would do such a thing."

Michael laughed to hide his embarrassment. "You mean you thought it was for women alone?"

"Sí."

"Then," Michael said, forcing bravado in his voice, "I will enlighten you, señorita."

"Did you bring it?"

"My diary?"

"Sí! What else are we talking about."

"It's in my saddlebags."

"Mine is in the drawer by my bedside. I will read a page to you if you will read some pages to me."

"I don't know," Michael said. "I have never shown the pages of it to anyone."

"I will be kind. You do not have to read the pages most from your heart. Read me the ones written in happiness."

"There are very few."

Aurora looked up at Michael's face. "Maybe that will change, señor."

Feeling his heart skip a little as they passed out of the courtyard, Michael said, "Maybe."

Ten

"THE END," Aurora said, closing the old worn book softly and then gazing deeply into Michael's eyes. "So now you know something of the great heart of Don Quixote told by a Spaniard, Miguel de Cervantes."

"He was a brilliant novelist and you are a fine reader, señorita."

Aurora laughed and Michael knew she was delighted by his simple but heartfelt comment. In the past three days it had become painfully obvious to him that he was grossly deficient in his knowledge of literature and history, while Aurora was a highly educated young woman. She had spent three years in Madrid studying to become a nun but at the last minute decided to return to California.

"I have no regrets," she had said. "I have been happy here with my father, and the land is beautiful."

Now, with the last soft rays of sunlight lancing through the slats in the arbor, Aurora reached out with her hand. "We sit too much. Come, let us take a walk, Michael."

He was only too happy to oblige Aurora, as he had on each of the two previous evenings. Around noon the sky had filled with clouds and there had been a sudden downpour, with ominous rolling thunder and jittering bolts of lightning. But the storm had raced east over the Sierras, leaving the huge valley smelling earthy. Now, as the sun appeared, the oak trees steamed and the withered brown grass glistened.

Aurora led Michael out into the valley to the banks of a little creek.

"The earth is so beautiful after the rain," Aurora said happily. "It has a new freshness that cleanses my soul and refreshes my spirit."

"You are the one that refreshes my spirit," Michael confessed.

She stopped and turned to look at him. "Joaquín said that he must return to his cabin tomorrow. I would like you to stay here awhile."

"Why?"

"Do you really need to ask such a question?"

"I don't know," he said. "I'm starting to get all mixed up inside. I think of you and of Tessa, sometimes both at the same time."

She came to his side and took his hand. "There is a lifetime to think but only a few precious years to love and feel deeply. We should not waste a moment of them."

"We've both been hurt," he said, avoiding her eyes.

She released his hand. "And you still will not let me read your diary, even though I read you six pages of mine?"

He had to smile. "You only read me the parts about how you helped that young woman have her baby. And about how much you love the filly and your father, but not in that order."

"So? It is more than you will tell me about yourself."

"There is not much to tell. I was a man of great dreams, but not anymore."

She started to protest. He leaned forward and lightly kissed her lips before he backed away, adding, "I'm really not."

Michael took Aurora's hand and continued walking. He was not sure what he wanted to say, only that he felt like talking. "I loved Tessa Glynn so deeply that I'm still numb inside. Some days I do fine, but other days I find myself almost lost in memories. I don't have anything to speak of, only a good horse and saddle and a few dollars in the bank at Sacramento. I may never have anything or even want anything. I'm not a man to count on, Aurora."

"You need time," she said. "How much time?"

"I don't know. Maybe a year." Michael stopped and turned to her. "How long has it been since you and Joaquín were . . . close?"

"Two years."

"Does it get easier?"

"Every day," she told him. "I laugh now and sing. I think mostly about good things. I take pleasure in the company of my father and am glad that I am here to comfort him in his last days. He does not show it, Michael, but he is very weak. You should have seen him even ten years ago. He was muy hombre, I tell you."

"I'll just bet he was."

"Ask Joaquín sometime about my father. He will tell you stories that you will not believe. And when my father is gone, it will be the end of something that will never return."

Michael frowned. "Endings are meant for beginnings. The old people always think their time was the best. Maybe it was, but maybe not."

"It was. In days of the Californios there was grace and prosperity and happiness. A man was judged by his generosity and the goodness of his heart, not by the size of his rancho or his herds. Even poor men had dignity. The vaquero never had a thing except his skill, his pride, devotion and his string of horses. It was enough then, but now, now the gold has changed everything—and not in a good way."

Michael could not argue with the woman. He'd passed through hundreds of strikes and witnessed the gold fever in men's eyes. He'd seen beggars and thieves and whores and men lost in mind and spirit, weeping because they would never return to their families and would die alone in California, broke and unloved.

"But enough of this," Aurora said, forcing gaiety into her voice. "We will walk to touch the sunset, then return for a great meal. And tomorrow you can decide if you will leave with Joaquín."

"Perhaps I would like to stay," he began, "but . . ."

"Then you will stay!" she cried, squeezing his hand and tugging him forward into a playful run through the tall brown grass.

Michael made his decision then. He *would* stay.

THAT NIGHT Michael went to bed early, but because he had consumed too much wine and eaten too heavily, he could not sleep, even when the hour grew late. He thought of Aurora and of Tessa. Their faces floated before his eyes and they both spoke to him, but their words were a jumble and the air in his room seemed heavy, damp and oppressive.

Sometime after midnight he felt the need to relieve himself, so he climbed out of bed and, without bothering to pull on his boots, moved down the dark hallway.

Michael stopped before a door that opened to the courtyard. Something, perhaps a sound, perhaps a little motion, had caught his attention. Then he stepped out a few feet into the moonlit courtyard. A moment later he staggered backward and leaned against the adobe wall. His hand brushed across his face. He blinked, unwilling to trust his vision.

Joaquín was holding Aurora in his arms and they were gazing into each other's eyes, speaking softly to one another. Michael could not decipher their Spanish whispers or see the expression on their faces. He heard only the gentle sound of their voices and saw their profiles, both strong and Castilian proud.

Michael turned quickly and hurried back down the hallway to his room. There was a chamber pot under his bed that the maid would empty in the morning. It was his great curse that he had not already thought to use it.

In the early morning, long before daylight, Michael slipped out of his room after a sleepless night and made his way out to the pasture. He caught Nugget, saddled the gelding, and galloped away without looking back at old Rancho San Pablo.

Michael had no real destination. He simply wanted to be rid

of Joaquín and Aurora, two crafty and deceitful lovers. He was finished with both of them. He knew he could not face either again.

It was just breaking daylight when Michael rode through Hornitos. He did not stop. He kept riding with some vague idea of passing back through Agua Fria and then striking a little to the northwest. He would return to the higher Sierras in search of quartz and the gold it attracted.

At midmorning Michael halted to let his horse drink from a stream. He was tired and his eyes burned from lack of sleep, while his heart ached with the pain of fresh deception.

"Amigo!"

Michael looked up and saw Joaquín racing his big gray stallion toward him, waving his arm. The vaquero was still a long way off and Michael meant to keep him at a distance. Jerking Nugget's head up, he spurred the gelding into a hard run.

Joaquín yelled all the louder and attempted to catch up. But while Nugget was still relatively fresh, Joaquín's horse had already run a great distance and was winded and tired. Even so, for the next five or six minutes the vaquero actually gained ground. Then his horse began to falter and he drew in on his reins.

Michael left the vaquero far behind. Skirting Agua Fria, he headed north. Dusk found him leaving the valley oaks and riding into pine forests.

That night Michael made a cold camp beside an even colder Sierra river. He had not bothered to stop for supplies and had no food, but he wasn't hungry. Long, long after dark he stared into his campfire, his thoughts dark and brooding.

Michael was just about to lie down and sleep when he suddenly heard a horse crashing through brush. Reaching for the gun at his side, Michael staggered to his feet in time to see Joaquín Murieta burst out of the forest, reata whirling in his hand.

"Joaquín!"

One word was all that Michael had time to utter before the

leather reata settled over his shoulders, pinning his arms to his side as Joaquín's horse sailed over his campfire and back into the trees. When Joaquín's horse struck the end of the reata, Michael felt himself being torn from the earth and hurled forward. He landed on a bed of pine needles, howled with pain as his body slammed and then ricocheted off a log and went spinning down the bank of the river.

As freezing as it was, the water was a blessing after being dragged across rocks and through brush. Michael tried to holler in protest, but the reata squeezed the air from his lungs. He could not get out a word as he was pulled underwater. He would have drowned if the river had been deep and wide, but as it was, he simply swallowed a bucketful and then struck a sandy bar on the other side before the vaquero yanked his horse to a standstill and dismounted.

Coughing, choking and cursing, Michael tried to stand. Joaquín slammed a boot down on his throat and put enough weight on it to bring him to silence.

"What the hell is the matter with you?" Joaquín demanded with barely controlled fury. "Why do you run out on me and our friends!"

Clenching his fists at his sides, Michael shouted, "I saw you embracing Aurora last night in the courtyard! What kind of a fool did you think I was to be tricked by the two of you that way!"

Joaquín cursed and dragged Michael to his feet. He drove a fist into Michael's belly, doubling him up, and then he smashed him in the back of the neck, dropping him back to the gravel.

"We did not betray you, Gringo fool! Do you think I would make love to another woman behind Rosita's back? Do you think Señorita López would ever betray you that way?"

Michael tore the reata from his body. Staggering to his feet, he glared at Joaquín. "Are you trying to tell me that you were holding that woman in the moonlight as a *friend?*"

The rage washed out of the vaquero. He stared at Michael for a moment, then his shoulders slumped and he said, "No, Amigo.

Not as a friend. But not as a lover either. Something . . . something in between.''

"I don't understand that," Michael said, with confusion. "Can you make me understand?"

"No."

"That's what I thought," Michael said, shivering and in pain. "So just leave me alone. Go back to your woman and your claim and your people and leave me alone. I don't understand any of you."

"That is very sad," Joaquín said as he coiled his reata and moved to his horse. "You have insulted not only the señorita but also myself."

Joaquín climbed onto his horse, took one last look at Michael, then rode back across the river and disappeared into the trees.

Eleven

WITH THE APPROACH of winter, many of the prospectors were building cabins or heading off for Stockton and Sacramento in the hope of finding jobs and making another stake that would enable them to resume prospecting next spring.

Alone and in low spirits, Michael rode aimlessly from one mining camp to another, never really taking an interest in his surroundings. Over and over he relived the nightmare of Joaquín embracing Aurora in her moonlit courtyard. The memory became even more painful as Michael realized that he had wronged his young Mexican friends. After all, if they were still lovers, wouldn't they have gone to the privacy of a room or at least sought privacy out in the meadow?

It did not help when Michael recalled the terrible fury that had been in Joaquín's eyes at their parting. And even worse, Aurora, who was smart and intuitive, would also understand his reason for having left Rancho San Pablo like a thief in the night. She must be deeply wounded and justifiably outraged. So, once again, Michael felt as if he had betrayed his dearest friends. First Paddy Ryan, now Aurora and Joaquín. Michael's guilt was boundless, overshadowed only by his sense of isolation.

November found Michael just outside Hangtown and he knew he could not turn his horse around without making an attempt to see Paddy. However, it was with considerable anxiety that he rode up to Paddy's Emporium and tied his weary horse. When Michael stepped inside, he asked a young clerk where he might find Paddy.

"Mr. and Mrs. Ryan have moved down to Sacramento. Can I be of any assistance?"

"No, thanks," Michael said. "I think I could find my way up and down these aisles in the dark."

The clerk looked at him quizzically, but Michael did not bother to explain. "How are they doing these days?"

"Very well, sir! Besides this store and the bigger one in Sacramento, Mr. Ryan is opening up new stores in both Stockton and Marysville."

"Paddy must be doing very well for himself."

"Oh yes, sir! And this was where he started." The clerk rubbed the worn top of his counter with reverence, as if it deserved some historical recognition. "Mr. Ryan first sold goods right here across this very counter."

"Yeah, I know. He was smarter than I was, and that's why he quit prospecting." Michael turned to leave.

"Sir?"

"Yes?"

"Can I give Mr. Ryan your name? He always likes to keep track of his friends."

Michael considered this for a moment, then shook his head. "Maybe I'll just ride over to Sacramento and pay him and his wife a visit. We grew up in the same New York Irish neighborhood."

"Really."

"Yes. We even came here on the same boat together—the *Orion.*"

The young man stared. "Then you *must* be Michael Callahan!"

"I am."

The clerk's eyes filled with respect and he said, "Mr. Ryan still talks about you."

"Frankly, I can't imagine why. What about Alfred? Is he still in Paddy's employ?"

"Oh yes, sir! Mr. Jenkins is in charge of new operations. He will be the one that oversees our Stockton and Marysville stores."

"Then what is Paddy doing?"

The clerk smiled apologetically. "Mr. Ryan is involved in many things these days. I'm afraid you'll have to ask him if you want specifics."

"I will," Michael said on his way outside.

THE NEXT AFTERNOON found Michael in Sacramento, riding up Ninth Street past the City Plaza, with its bronzed plaque reminding everyone that the Plaza was donated by John Augustus Sutter. His first stop was at the Bank of California, where the bank manager failed to recognize him in his dusty riding clothes. Always before, Michael had been Mr. Ryan's partner, and now that he was no longer managing the store or wore a new suit, white shirt, collar and tie, Michael sensed a distinctly cooler reception.

"Here you go, Mike. One thousand and fifty-two dollars even and your account at this bank is terminated," the bank manager said.

"Closed. The word is closed, not terminated."

"Either way," the banker said, turning and walking away.

With cash money, Michael bought a shave, haircut, bath and a new set of clothes. He was in need of a heavy winter jacket and some woolen underwear and blankets. For these he went to Paddy's store. Fortunately, his old friend was minding the store. When Michael walked in the door, Paddy rushed forward with outstretched arms.

"Mike, good to see you again!"

"Michael," he corrected. "And it's good to see you again too, Paddy. How have you and the Missus been?"

"Getting fatter and richer every day."

"I can see the first part plain enough," Michael said with a laugh, pointing to Paddy's double chins.

"Pearl is at some social affair all afternoon, but let's go for a walk or somewhere we can eat."

"Let's do both," Michael said.

Paddy, as Michael surmised, had a restaurant in mind, and they ordered a full meal of steaks, potatoes and sourdough bread.

"Like it?" Paddy asked. "Best steaks in Sacramento."

"Best I've ever eaten," Michael said, wiping up the last speck of his gravy with a piece of his bread.

"If you're still hungry, I'll order another steak for you," Paddy said.

"No, thanks." Michael leaned back in his chair and sipped his burgundy wine. He had not eaten this well since the last time he and Paddy had dined, and he probably wouldn't again for a good long while. "So tell me about these new stores."

"Oh, did you meet young Thomas Heath?"

"Yes. He sure sings your praises."

Paddy waved his hand with indifference, but it was easy to see that he was pleased. "Thomas is a good young man. He'll do well. As for the new emporiums, well, if I don't do it, others will."

"I thought you were going to be the mayor of Hangtown."

"Nah," Paddy grunted, signaling the waiter and then ordering apple pie for them both. "I've got my eye on bigger fish now."

"What? The mayor of Sacramento?"

"Why not?" Paddy asked expansively. "Did you know that, at this very moment, the United States Congress is in the process of authorizing money to conduct a study for a transcontinental railroad?"

"You don't say."

"I *do* say! And—mark my words, Mike—it will connect this country, and its western terminus will be right here in Sacramento. That will really put this city on the map. I have been assured that we will also win the state capitol in the next year or two."

Michael whistled softly. "So the mayor would be a pretty big deal."

"To put it mildly." Paddy glanced around to make sure that there were no eavesdroppers before he leaned forward and whispered, "I'm in good with the governor. Real good. He's given me a commission, Mike. Not only am I on several key committees to consider the routing of the transcontinental railroad into California, but I'm head of the Commerce Commission."

"Sounds important." Michael was beginning to feel disquieted and a little restless. He decided that he would suggest a walk after dessert.

"It is very important," Paddy said. "In my opinion, California and especially Sacramento are going to be international trade centers."

"Is that a fact?"

"That's right. How long did it take us to reach California on that miserable ship, the *Orion?"*

"Almost six months."

"Well," Paddy said, steepling his pudgy fingers together, "the *Flying Cloud,* a fast Yankee clipper, covered the same seas in less than eighty-two days! And sail is on the way out. Steam is the future, Michael! It will drive locomotives over the Sierras, and it will bring goods and take our agricultural produce out to feed the world."

Michael shook his head. "I always said you were a man of vision."

Paddy drew one of his expensive cigars and instantly the waiter was at his side to light it for him. Puffing contentedly, Paddy said, "Michael, it's killing me to watch you go nowhere in life."

Michael bristled. "I like to chart my own course."

"I am painfully aware of that fact," Paddy said, "but sometimes we need a little extra wind behind our sails. I know all the people in this town that can help you do just about anything you want." Paddy stopped for a moment and resumed, almost pleading now. "Just tell me what you want to do!"

"I don't know anymore," Michael said quietly, "but if I ever figure it out, you'll be the second to know, right after myself."

Paddy sighed deeply. "Do you still write in that diary of yours?"

"Yep. I'm on the third one."

"I don't suppose you'd let me read them someday."

"Why?" Michael demanded. "So that you can see how fast I'm going nowhere?"

"Of course not! I was just thinking that . . ." Paddy waved his cigar. "Never mind."

"Spit it out."

"I was just thinking that, since you write so well and it seems to be the only constant in your life, you might enjoy becoming a newspaperman. A journalist at first, then a publisher. I could introduce you to a few men who might want to back some kind of literary effort."

"I have no idea what you're talking about."

"Neither do I," Paddy said, quite miserably. "I was just thinking about some chronicle of the gold camps. Maybe it would sell and you could earn a tidy profit. Or a newsletter or something."

"You're really fishing for something, aren't you?" Michael said, coming to his feet and dragging out his bank money.

"No, no! I'll pay."

"I insist. How much?"

"I don't know. Why don't we wait for the check?"

But Michael was seething with impatience and torn between his sincere caring for Paddy and the uneasiness the man caused him whenever they were together. Back in the old days, they'd been equals—both with dreams, both without funds. Now—now Michael could not help but feel inferior whenever he was with Paddy, even if the man was doing his damnedest to help him succeed at something.

"Will fifty dollars cover it?"

"That's more than enough," Paddy said, coming heavily to his feet. "But I wish that—"

"If only just this once," Michael said, "let *me* pay the bill. Okay?"

"Sure," Paddy said as he threw his napkin down on the table and headed for the door.

Outside, they walked in silence back to the emporium and went inside by the counter. "I better be riding."

"Think about what I said."

"Sure."

"At least take care of those diaries. Someday they're going to be very valuable. Mark my words, they'll have commercial value."

"For me they already have value."

Michael started to leave in anger but Paddy's hand stopped him. "Listen, I'm sorry if I offended you. It's just that I wish you and I could see each other more. That we could be partners again."

"What you do," Michael said with resignation, "I can't do. And what I can do, you don't want to do. Does that make any sense?"

"Yes, I'm afraid it does. But I always feel better in your company. I need someone I can really trust."

"You can trust Pearl."

"I know that, but sometimes a man's friendship is needed."

Michael felt a lump rising in his throat. "I could use a friend too," he admitted, "but I don't suppose that Pearl would take it too well if we ran off and wintered in the mountains."

"No," Paddy said, "she would not. We'd like to have a baby. Did I tell you that last time?"

"Uh-uh," Michael said, "but I think it's a fine idea. You'd make wonderful parents."

"We think so. What about you, Michael?" Paddy asked suddenly. "Are you getting over Miss Glynn?"

"Yes." Very quickly Michael told him a few things about Aurora and Joaquín and how he'd ruined that friendship.

"Don't get involved with the Mexicans," Paddy advised sternly. "They're too different and you'll never understand them."

"I guess not," Michael said, a little disappointed by his friend's remark. "But Joaquín Murieta considered me a very good friend."

"Maybe he wanted something."

Exasperated, Michael turned and pointed to the street. "Do you see that horse tied out in front?"

"Sure."

"He was a gift of Joaquín. Saddle and bridle, too."

Paddy looked skeptical but said, "I guess there are good Mexicans among the bad. I would just hate to see you get involved with a Mexican woman, that's all."

Thoroughly disgusted, Michael headed out the door. "I've got to go."

"I've made you mad, have I?" Paddy asked as he followed Michael outside and watched him mount his gelding. "Mike, say something."

"All right. You just made me realize that what I need to do is make amends. And I'm doing that right now."

Michael reached down from his saddle and extended his hand. "I'm sorry I ran out on you and this store. I realized that Alfred was a better man for the job."

"That's true in some ways," Paddy said, "but not all. Alfred is a good manager with a sense for making a dollar, but the customers don't much like him. Now you, well, I still have people asking me if you'll ever come back and work here."

"Is that a fact?" Secretly, Michael was very gratified by this news.

"It is," Paddy said. "You had a way with customers. They liked you and they came back with their business. That kind of goodwill is hard to put a value on, though it might just be the most important attribute any storekeeper needs to keep customers and stay in business."

"It's nice to hear you say that, Paddy."

"Well, I mean it. I'd find a place for you in my business this instant if I thought it would make you happy."

"Tending a store wouldn't," Michael said, gripping his friend's hand, "but seeing you prosper makes me happy indeed."

Paddy seemed reluctant to release Michael's hand, and his round face was somber. "I don't think I'll tell Pearl you were in town. She'd be hurt that you didn't stop by to see her."

"I will next time," Michael promised. "And next time, I expect to discover you're a father."

"We've already decided to name our first son Mike, after you."

"I'm flattered, Paddy. I really am. But I'd hope he would be more practical than me—that he'd have your business sense."

Paddy stepped back and smoothed his vest, his thick fingers absently brushing the heavy gold watch chain. "You come by again soon. Pearl and I will treat you to a dinner you won't forget."

"Haven't forgotten the last one," Michael said as he smiled and rode south, determined to make amends first with Joaquín, then with Aurora López.

Arriving in Jamestown, Michael learned that the same geologist he'd listened to a year earlier was speaking, and he paid a pinch of gold worth a dollar to hear him again. This time, however, the geologist was a little drunk and he said nothing about quartz but instead talked about how each new spring runoff brought more gold tumbling down the rivers and also washed away deposits hidden in gullies and ravines. The geologist even had elaborate drawings showing big gold nuggets protruding from new and deepened gullies washed out by the snow-fed streams.

To Michael the lecture was quite disappointing, even though it was obvious that the geologist had learned to satisfy the crowd far better by offering them fresh hope. After the talk Michael was able to pull the geologist aside and say, "What about last year and the lecture on quartz?"

The man stared at him without recognition. "What about it?"

"You said quartz bonded with gold. Find the first, you'll likely find the latter."

"Did I?"

Michael stared into the man's bloodshot eyes. He reeked of whiskey. "I liked you better when you used big words. At least you were honest."

"You want quartz?" the man challenged. "Head up the North Fork of the Cosumnes River! That's where I spent this year pecking around at a mountain of quartz. Fat damn lot of good it did me or anyone else who'd listened to my theories. Why, I was almost lynched by July!"

Michael started to relate his own experience with gold and quartz, but someone jammed a bottle of whiskey into the geologist's fist and led him away.

Two days later Michael rode through Agua Fria and then cut east up into the mountains. By the time he came in sight of Joaquín's cabin, his stomach was churning with nerves, but he was determined to at least try to make amends. The cabin, however, was occupied by three white men who were just sitting down to an outside meal.

"Have a plate and a cup of coffee with us, stranger," the tallest one said, stroking his beard and studying Michael's fine horse and saddle.

Michael declined. He well remembered the last time that he'd put himself at the mercy of three strangers, and these miners looked hard and mean-spirited.

"Maybe some other time," he said, noting how Rosita's herb garden had been trampled and allowed to die from neglect. That was a pity, because Rosita had always taken especially great pride in growing medicinal herbs. Once, she had spent more than an hour showing Michael her garden and explaining that her yerba buena, or common mint, was used for tea or to flavor menudo, a tripe stew. Yerba mansa, when chewed, would relieve colds. Yerba del pasmo was a poultice to draw out poisons, while hojasen was very good as a physic. Ruda, when picked and crushed, could relieve the itchiness of poison ivy or oak, and azafran was used in bath water by the old to cure rheumatism.

"Hey!" the man growled, pulling Michael's attention from Rosita's devastated herb garden. "What do you want here?"

"I'm looking for a man named Joaquín Murieta."

The tall man stopped stroking his beard and glanced at his friends before he looked back at Michael. "What for? He owe you for something?"

"No. I owe him."

"You *owe* a Mexican?" the man asked, as if he had heard incorrectly.

"That's right. You know where he and his wife are now?"

"Well, we done drove them the hell off this claim about two weeks ago. Run him off at the point of a gun."

Michael was angry but not surprised. Running Mexicans and Chinese off their rightful claims was commonplace in the gold country, but it was unlike Joaquín to leave without a fight.

"You must have caught Joaquín by surprise then," Michael said. "Either that, or you had more help than I see you have now."

A man whose bald head seemed to sit directly on his bull shoulders spat tobacco juice between Nugget's front feet and said, "Mister, you got something to say, make it plain."

Michael decided nothing could be gained by staying here. He started to rein his horse away, but the tall man acted like he was going to grab Nugget's bit, so Michael yanked his gun out of his holster, catching them by surprise.

"You boys just go back to your eating," he warned.

The three men stiffened and looked to the tall one, who hissed, "You're a damn Mexican-lover, ain't ya!"

"Yeah, I guess I get along with most of them just fine."

The third man, who had not spoken yet, said, "I seen you once in Columbia and a man told me the Mexicans called you the Gringo Amigo or some such damn thing. Is that right?"

"It is."

"Well, I call you a garbage to your own kind."

It was a good thing that Michael had the drop on them because they were all wearing sidearms and it looked as if they were in a sweat to use them.

"Keep your hands away from your guns," Michael ordered, backing his own horse away from Joaquín's cabin.

When he had some distance between them, he started to whirl his horse around, but the third man shouted, "If we see either you or that Mexican again, we'll kill you both without warning!"

"I'll remember that," Michael called as he reined Nugget around and sent his horse racing off into the cover of the forest.

Back in Agua Fria, Michael did what he should have done from the start, and that was to ask a Mexican where the Murieta family had gone.

"A place called Murphy's, Señor Gringo Amigo."

"That's just above Angel's Camp. Tell me, señor, was Joaquín beaten, or just run off at gunpoint?"

The Mexican simply shrugged his shoulders, and Michael did not waste any more time as he reined north.

He arrived at Murphy's early the following afternoon. The settlement was named after John and Dan Murphy, who'd discovered gold two years before. However, there hadn't been another local gold strike here and Michael supposed that was why Joaquín had chosen this place, hoping that the gringos would leave him and Rosita in peace. Most of the stores were either boarded up or falling down, but there were still a few in business.

"Say," he called to a man sitting on a chair outside the barbershop. "Can you tell me where the Murieta family lives?"

"Joaquín and that pretty little gal of his live up the mountain about five miles. He deals poker here at one of the fandango halls when he ain't stealin' horses."

"He's not a horse thief."

"I figure that a hangman will prove you wrong one of these days," the man said. "We hung his brother a few years ago and we'll do the same to him."

Michael was stunned. Joaquín had never said anything about a brother being hanged.

It wasn't hard to find Joaquín and Rosita's little cabin nestled against a steep mountainside. The vaquero's fine gray stallion was hobbled in a large meadow, and when it saw Nugget it lifted its head and bugled a challenge.

Nugget whinnied in return, but Michael said, "Just let it pass. That big stallion would eat you alive, my friend."

Joaquín stepped out of the cabin, a rifle to his shoulder.

"Hey!" Michael called. "It's me! Don't shoot!"

Joaquín lowered the rifle, and Rosita stepped out to join him. Michael did not see the smile he'd hoped for on the vaquero's lips, but he guessed that had been unrealistic. Joaquín's appearance had changed dramatically. He was still very handsome, but he had lost his boyish good looks. His eyes were hooded and his features more chiseled. He appeared to be as thin as a winter-starved wolf.

Michael removed his hat. "I have come to make my apologies for acting like such a fool."

Joaquín dropped the butt of his rifle beside his boot. "Your apology is accepted," he said stiffly. "Unsaddle and then hobble your horse before you join us for something to eat."

Michael did as he was ordered. He trudged over to the stream and saw that the Murietas had moved a great deal of rock and gravel through a sluice box that was at least forty feet long. Michael knelt by the stream and removed his shirt. He splashed water on his face, arms and torso while Joaquín stood close by with his rifle in his fists.

"You act like you are expecting big trouble," Michael said.

"A man who does not expect trouble is a fool, Gringo."

"I went to your old claim looking for you. Instead, I found three men."

"There were five," Joaquín said, but he did not elaborate.

"Did you kill the other two?" Michael asked without thinking. He quickly added, "I am sorry. That is none of my business."

"That is true."

"Look," Michael said, "I acted like a jealous, stupid fool at Rancho San Pablo. I know that. I deserved being roped, dragged and punched. I know that too. And I'm sorry."

Joaquín almost smiled. "How come you know so much all of a sudden, Amigo?"

"Now *that* I don't know." Michael scooped up a handful of sand and sorted it with his forefinger, hunting for a trace of color. Finding none, he tossed it into the stream and said, "Are you and Rosita finding any gold here?"

"Some."

Michael guessed it couldn't be very much, because there were no extra horses and the vaquero's pants were patched at the knees, his boots worn to nothing.

"I was wondering if you might want to join me in looking for gold up on the Cosumnes River. I heard there is a lot of quartz rock up that way."

"There is no money in quartz."

"You know my meaning. Interested?"

Joaquín shrugged in a way that suggested he did not have an opinion. His dark eyes returned to the line of forest trees. "I have some troubles here."

"What kind of troubles?"

"*Gringo* troubles."

"That's all the more reason to leave."

When Joaquín said nothing, Michael finished washing and dried himself with his shirt, then dipped it into the stream, rubbed it around in the sand and wrung it out to dry. He stood up, went over to his saddlebags and took out a clean shirt. He could smell tortillas cooking and probably some beans and chilis, too.

"It's good to see you and Rosita again," Michael said. "When I saw you step outside with that rifle, well, I wasn't sure what kind of a greeting I'd receive."

"Like I say," Joaquín told him, "I am expecting trouble."

"And like I said, all the more reason for you and Rosita to

leave this place and come with me. If we're partners the gringos won't bother you."

Joaquín barked a laugh that had no mirth. "So, now *you* would protect *me?*"

"That isn't the way I meant it and you know it."

Joaquín dropped his cigarette and ground the butt under his heel. "Come and eat," he ordered. "You are even skinnier than me."

After eating, Joaquín rolled a cigarette and walked outside to sit on a rock. Rosita, who had said little during the meal, stayed inside, leaving the two men to talk alone in the yard.

"She's mad at me for even thinking you would cheat on her, isn't she?" Michael said, glancing over his shoulder.

Joaquín nodded his head, smoke curling lazily from his nostrils, the Winchester resting easy in his left hand.

"I'll apologize to her again and again. I'll make amends to her somehow."

"Don Luis López died last week," Joaquín said, looking westward toward the valley.

"So soon?"

"Uh-huh."

Michael stuffed his hands into his pockets. "I am sorry to hear this. He was a good man. So now what will happen to Aurora?"

"She is leaving the rancho. That was the agreement. I do not know where she will live. Maybe Hornitos or Agua Fria. Perhaps even in Sonora, where she has many friends."

Michael nodded. "I will pay my respects to her soon."

"Maybe she could come with us," Joaquín said, suddenly looking into Michael's eyes and challenging him with the question.

"I don't think so," Michael said, after a moment.

Joaquín flipped his cigarette into the water, grabbed a shovel and began pitching wet sand and gravel into the sluice box. Michael grabbed a second shovel. They worked in a hard silence until the sun lowered itself behind the treetops. Michael didn't think that they had enough gold trapped behind the riffle bars to bother with, but Joaquín and Rosita painstakingly searched for gold flakes and nuggets until they could no longer see.

That night Joaquín talked of his days when he was a real vaquero. "I miss it very much, but when the gringos came, the Mexican cattle and horse ranches were lost and work for a vaquero was over."

"You could find a vaquero's work in Mexico," Michael said, sensing Joaquín's loss of purpose and dignity and how much he disliked prospecting.

"Of course," Joaquín agreed, "but I like money too much to live poor. I am spoiled now and . . . I have Rosita. Maybe a big family to take care of someday, eh?"

"I'm sure."

"Ah, Amigo, but I was not made for grubbing in cold mountain streams. Do you know what I was thinking about all this day?"

"No."

"I was remembering how I used to colear—tail, as you say in English—the wild bulls."

"Tail them?"

"Sí." Joaquín pointed out toward his gray stallion. "On that very horse."

"But why the tail?"

Joaquín shrugged. "As the gringos say, 'for the hell of it,' I guess. Anyway, only a few vaqueros can do it well, and I was one of them. But you must have a brave horse. One that will rush close to the rear of the bull so that the coleador can reach down and grab the tail at its very end. Then, gripping it strongly between your horse and leg, you must turn the horse and throw the bull off his hind feet."

"It sounds dangerous. What if the bull flips in front of your horse?"

"This," Joaquín admitted, "can happen—even to me. But do you know what I most feared?"

"What?"

Joaquín blew out his cheeks and made the sound of a loud

passing of wind. His handsome face twisted in revulsion, he snapped his right hand several times, then laughed. "Sometimes, when you pull the tail, the bull will have *another* kind of accident. Comprende, Amigo?"

Michael understood completely and thought how good it was to see Joaquín laugh again.

"You see this reata?" Joaquín asked as he walked over and retrieved it from a peg on his wall.

"Sure."

"You can judge the quality of a cowboy or a vaquero by the rope he uses. Now a fine reata like this must be made from the hide of a steer of exactly the right age and condition—and when the moon is full."

"Full?"

"Sí, it's true. And the hide must be removed very carefully. If the knife slices it too thin, then the whole thing is no good. And the reata must always be braided in winter, not in the summer, because the rawhide dries out too fast in the heat. I prefer cattle raised by the sea, never in the desert. It is only when the hide is damp, a little green, eh, that the braids can be pulled tightly together."

Michael studied the reata with real interest. "Did you make that one?"

"Of course. It is the finest that I have ever seen. I have roped many bulls and cattle."

"What about the grizzly?"

"Two grizzly, but not with this rope, because their claws might ruin it."

"I'd never even try to become a roper."

"It is just as well. To do it right you must learn as a boy. It is hard. A real vaquero can rope a bull and lay it down on the earth as gently as a mother does a babe in its cradle. And there is an old saying that the hondo commands the loop, the loop the coils, and the throw is decided by the way one whirls and casts. It is very difficult."

"And you miss it very, very much," Michael said.

Joaquín nodded sadly, his long, slender brown fingers caressing the braids of his reata, unconsciously inspecting every inch.

"Someday when I am rich," Joaquín mused out loud, "I will buy a ranch and rope cattle again instead of chickens, dogs and cats."

Michael looked into the Mexican's face and thought he saw amusement, and perhaps also remembered the disgust of Don Luis that afternoon at Rancho San Pablo.

For hours after that, Joaquín talked about the life of the vaquero, much like old Don Luis, and Michael was struck by their similarities. Both seemed to be men out of their time and natural place in life.

Finally, when Michael's eyelids were drooping, he grabbed his bedroll and headed outside to sleep under a tree.

"Amigo?"

Michael turned around at the edge of the yard.

Joaquín stood in his doorway. "In the morning we will leave this place and go to the quartz. At least there," Joaquín said, "we can starve among pretty rocks."

Michael smiled with relief, knowing Joaquín was no longer angry with him. "Yeah," he said, "only we'll do a lot better than today."

"How do you know this?" Joaquín asked, folding his arms across his chest.

"I just have a hunch."

Joaquín considered this for several moments, then he nodded, turned and closed the door to his cabin, leaving Michael to stand alone in the yard gazing out into the dark, star-studded heavens and wondering what the hell good was a "hunch" about anything. Every prospector in the gold fields had a "hunch" he was going to strike it rich. It was always a "hunch" that hooked him into believing the very next claim he staked would finally be the big one.

Hunches. Michael guessed that they were as important to a Forty-Niner as the air he breathed, and worth about as much at the general store.

Twelve

MICHAEL HEARD Joaquín's stallion trumpet in the darkness, but he did not fully wake until the cold steel of a gun barrel was pressed against his temple and the sudden light of a match exploded before his eyes.

"He's a white man!"

"He's a greaser-lover," another voice sneered in the darkness.

Michael tried to sit up, but a second and very painful light exploded across his consciousness, only this one was *behind* his eyes. For several moments he was stunned, his body quivering like that of a dying animal, and he could neither speak nor think nor act—only hear faraway voices.

"Let's go! I've been wanting to get that uppity Murieta once and for all."

"What about this one? I ain't gonna kill him. Killin' a white man—even a Mex-lover—would raise a real stink in these parts. Bad enough what we got planned for the woman."

Michael dimly heard a curse, and then he was rolled over onto his stomach. His arms were jerked up behind his back and he was tied at the wrists and ankles.

"Hit him again! We can't afford no witnesses."

Something in the dim recesses of his mind caused Michael to struggle violently, and when the butt of a pistol connected against his skull, it was a glancing blow, but it was enough to drop him into total darkness.

JOAQUÍN AWOKE with a start, but the familiar cocking of a Winchester rifle froze him in his bed.

"Get 'em!"

Joaquín heard Rosita scream with fear. He reached for his gun, certain that these men would hang or shoot him, but if he were to die quickly before their blood was up, perhaps they would leave his wife alone. It was the hope of a desperate man.

When the rifle boomed in the close confines of their cabin, Joaquín felt a searing pain across his arm. An instant later he was yanked out of bed and dragged kicking and fighting outside into the yard.

"Tie the sonofabitch to that big pine tree over yonder and let's flog him to death!" a man shouted. "We'll use the greaser's own damn rawhide reata!"

"What about the woman?"

"We know how to treat that kind."

"No!" Joaquín cried as he was slammed against a tree and lashed to its rough bark. "No!"

Dimly he heard Rosita's screams from the cabin, and he fought the ropes like a crazy man. His shirt was ripped to expose his naked back and when the first blow whistled in the darkness and the rawhide bit into his flesh, an involuntary cry escaped Joaquín's distended mouth.

Again the reata whistled, and this time Joaquín clenched his teeth and his lean body pushed hard against the rough bark of the tree, but the effect was the same and he twisted and struggled helplessly.

"I'll kill you!" he choked in English so that they would understand.

"Not in this lifetime you won't!"

To disperse the pain from his back, Joaquín slammed his head feverishly against the rough bark until his forehead was matted with bark and blood. He gripped the tree with his arms and knees and held on to it with all his might.

Again and again the reata hissed its warning and then bit into his flesh, until Joaquín's legs buckled and he sagged heavily against the pine tree, held upright by the bloodied gringo grass ropes.

The flogging continued until much later, while he floated half-conscious, his body on fire and his mind drugged with pain.

"Jake!"

"No names, damn you!"

"But the Mex woman is *dead!*"

"What!"

"She had a knife. Used it, too! First on—"

"I said no names!"

Joaquín hung against the tree, gasping and fighting for air. His lungs burned and he could taste blood where he had bitten his tongue almost in half.

"Rosita," he whispered. Then louder, "Rosita!"

"I think we'd better get out of here!"

"Wait! We've got to use our heads!"

Joaquín heard them argue over his fate. He knew who they were, for he had recognized every voice. Five men and—if God believed in earthly justice—all would beg for death soon.

He must have lost consciousness because when he roused again, Joaquín felt himself being dragged back toward the cabin and dumped on the floor. He heard glass break and smelled kerosene and then he heard a great *whoosh* and felt searing heat.

"Let's get out of here!"

Joaquín forced himself to his hands and knees. Slowly he crawled to his bed, and when he saw what the men had done to Rosita, a cry of anguish and rage filled his throat. But with flames eating at the cabin, he had no time for grief. Joaquín dragged Rosita's violated body off their bed and to the door as he choked and gasped for air.

"Get him!" a voice across the yard called.

Through the smoke, Joaquín saw his tormentors open fire, and he dropped to the floor and rolled sideways, dragging Rosita's body out of the doorway, but not before she was hit several times. Cursing and screaming like a man insane, he pulled Rosita's body back deeper into the burning cabin.

There was no hope of putting out the fire and no hope of escape through the window or doorway. So now Joaquín dragged his dead wife over to the secret trapdoor he and Reyes Feliz had built in the floor. Sobbing, he knocked the table aside, brushed away the heavy woven horse blanket that served as a rug, and grabbed the inset door handle.

With all of his strength, Joaquín lifted the door and pushed Rosita down into the hole, then followed her, moving back into the narrow escape tunnel that ran up behind the cabin and into the forest.

He could feel the heat of the inferno above as it radiated down the tunnel. Sparks, then pieces of the burning floor began to collapse into his tunnel. He dragged Rosita's body farther and farther up into the mountainside until he could feel the cool night air telling him he was close beside the tunnel's exit, which was hidden in a clump of thick manzanita.

Joaquín pulled Rosita's body to his side and rocked back and forth. He laid his cheek against her cheek, weeping as he had not wept since losing his own parents many years ago. How long he remained holding Rosita and rocking back and forth he did not know. But finally, when her body was cold and her limbs were growing stiff, he left her in the tunnel and crawled out into the twilight of a new day.

Nothing remained of the cabin but a smoking ruin. The only thing still standing was the old barrel stove. In the meadow Joaquín's beloved stallion was gone, along with Michael's good sorrel gelding. Even his sluice box was torn apart and much of it had been swept away by the current. Joaquín stared at his bloody reata, which lay tangled at the base of a tree. Half out of his mind, he staggered around in a full circle to see Michael struggling against his bonds.

"Amigo!" he shouted.

His voice echoed up and down the hills and he stumbled forward. "Amigo!"

Michael raised his busted head. He spat dirt and pine needles, then tried to roll onto his back but failed.

"Joaquín!" he cried weakly.

The vaquero knelt by his side, and when Michael looked up at his friend's ravaged face, he ceased his struggles and stared with horror at his Mexican friend.

"Joaquín?"

"Sí."

Michael waited for the man to continue speaking or to cut his ropes or at least to show some kind of reaction. But the vaquero's face was blank, and the fact that he spoke without feeling made his words somehow all the more chilling.

"I will kill them all for taking the life of my Rosita," he said in very deliberate English. "I will kill them all and they will die screaming for mercy."

Rosita was dead. Somehow Michael had known it even last night, but his mind had been so filled with pain and helpless rage that he had not directly addressed Rosita's death until this very moment.

Unbidden, the trite words fell from his lips. "I'm sorry, Amigo. She was a beautiful woman, and I know that you loved her dearly, and . . ." Joaquín was not even listening.

Michael stopped without finishing. He realized how pathetic and hollow his words were. They held little comfort or meaning to Joaquín, and his own busted head was of no consequence compared to the death of the young Mexican woman. He did not even want to consider the circumstances of Rosita's death. One look at Joaquín told him all he needed or wanted to know.

"Please," he said, afraid that Joaquín was so benumbed that he might actually have lost his mind. "Untie me."

Joaquín untied him. He helped Michael up, and when the vaquero shuffled nearer to his cabin, Michael had to clench his teeth from gasping—the man's back was like a bloody side of beef.

The vaquero came to a halt near his smoking cabin and stood swaying. Michael followed him and said, "Do you know who they were?"

"Sí."

Michael waited. When he realized no answer was forthcoming, he said, "Please tell me."

Joaquín tore his eyes away from the smoking rubble of his cabin and looked deeply into Michael's eyes. "It is better if you do not know."

"What are you talking about? Don't you think *I* owe them something too?"

"Snyder. Rawlings. Bates. Moore. Blackman." Joaquín spat the words out one by one.

Michael's head ached so badly he cradled it in his hands. "All right," he whispered. "We'll find a sheriff."

Joaquín's laugh was terrible.

"I give you my word of honor that we'll find someone with the authority to arrest them," Michael swore. "There's a constable in Stockton."

Joaquín pivoted around, reached up and grabbed Michael's shoulders. "And what would you say when this 'constable' asked you who did this?"

"I would repeat the names you just gave me."

"And the constable, he would say, 'Did you see these men with your own eyes?' And you would say?"

"Well, no, not exactly."

"And then the constable would tell you to go away. He would say, 'If you have no proof, then do not bother me. And besides, only a Mexican woman was killed. And the Mexicans, as we know, have no more rights than dogs!'"

Michael shook his head. "I wouldn't let him say that, Joaquín. I would *insist* that he do something."

"No!"

Joaquín lowered his voice. "I want you to go away and leave me to bury my woman in peace."

"Let me help. She was my friend."

"No," Joaquín said, gently this time. "Go to Stockton and see the constable. You can give him the names and by the time he tells you that he can do nothing, at least one—maybe all of them —will be dead."

Michael watched as Joaquín turned away and shuffled down to the stream where the remains of his sluice box lay twisted and broken on the riverbank. The vaquero sagged to his knees in shallow water and then rocked forward, sinking down into the water with an audible gasp.

"Joaquín!"

The vaquero did not answer. Like a log, he floated out into the current, allowing the cold river water to ease the pain in his mutilated back. Michael twisted around in a full circle, searching for the shovels they had used the evening before. The shovels were gone, no doubt stolen. A shovel in this country was worth an ounce of gold.

"Joaquín! They also stole our horses! They can be hanged for that alone, Joaquín!"

But the vaquero did not answer. Instead, he rolled over onto his feet, crouching up to his neck in freezing cold water.

Michael did not know what to do. He did not know if Rosita's corpse lay smoldering in the ashes of the cabin, or where she might be. And since he could not even find a shovel, what could he do?

"I am going to Stockton then, Amigo! I will get there if I have to walk every step and I will bring back a sheriff who will arrest those animals. You will see, Joaquín! I swear that you will see!"

But Joaquín did *not* see, and even as Michael stumbled around and headed east toward the warm interior valley, he had the sick feeling inside that Joaquín Murieta would never see things quite the same way again.

THREE DAYS LATER, Michael half jumped and half fell off the back of a buckboard wagon in Stockton. Like Sacramento, the busy town was already looking more to agriculture than placer gold for its livelihood and future.

"You better see the doc before you see the sheriff, mister!" the buckboard driver yelled over his shoulder. "You need some help!"

Michael muttered his thanks for the meals and free transportation he'd received, but there was no warmth between himself and the driver. Earlier, when Michael had explained his mission, the buckboard driver had snorted, "Damn Mexicans ain't got no rights in California! They kicked out the Spaniards, took away their missions and their ranchos and now they think we ought to let 'em keep what *they* stole. No siree!"

Michael, despite the intense pain inside his head and a persistent double vision, had attempted to explain that it wasn't a case of history, it was a case of right versus wrong, justice as opposed to injustice. It came down to a man, a woman—human beings, for Chrissakes!

After that, he and the driver hadn't spoken a word until just now.

Michael had washed the blood from his scalp and face, but the pistol-whipping had left his forehead, ears and the flesh right down around his eyes purple. Everyone stared at him as he staggered dizzily into the sheriff's office.

"Well, holy hog fat!" the sheriff shouted, coming out of his chair along with a lean young deputy. "Mister, what happened?"

"May I sit down?" Michael asked, feeling sick and shaky.

"Why hell yes! Walt, give the man your chair!"

The deputy brought the chair over for Michael to sit in and then said, "Mister, someone just pistol-whipped the hell out of you, didn't they?"

"Yeah. That's why I'm here. I want you to arrest five men who stole our horses and killed a woman up near Agua Fria."

The sheriff leaned forward. "Killed a woman? What woman?"

"Her name was Rosita Murieta."

"A Mexican?" the deputy blurted.

Michael's head snapped up. "That's right. A Mexican. She was probably raped first and then either strangled or shot. I don't know."

"Then you didn't see it happen?"

"No."

"What about the horses and the men that stole them?"

Michael reached into his shirt pocket. "I wrote their names down. Here."

He showed them his list. The sheriff scowled. "I don't know any of these fellas. Maybe you better back up and come in the front door on this story."

Michael took a deep breath. Very slowly, trying to miss nothing, he told them every detail that he could remember, and when he was finished they said nothing.

"Well, Sheriff?"

The sheriff was fortyish, with a big paunch which he decided to scratch.

"Well, there ain't much I can do about this if you didn't see 'em either kill the Mex girl or steal your horses."

"Do you think I'm making this up?"

"Of course not. But you said yourself that the Mexican—this Joaquín Murieta fella—he's the one that told you their names. And he could have given you anybody's name and you'd have no way to tell if it was true or not."

"You can't arrest someone on that kind of evidence," the deputy said, looking at the sheriff and nodding his head wisely.

"That's right," the sheriff said in his most reasonable tone of voice. Then he stood up and walked heavily over to the back of his office. "Mister, I think the thing for you to do right now is go find a doctor."

Michael jumped out of his seat, and the sudden movement caused a piercing pain to impale his skull. He groaned, grabbing his head.

"Walt, get him over to Doc Evans right now!"

The deputy grabbed Michael's arm, but he threw it aside and shouted, "Then you're not going to do a thing, right? It's going to be just like Joaquín said it would be—*no justice!*"

The sheriff's cheeks reddened. "No evidence is what we have

here, mister! Now you just go along with Walt and get that head looked at. You're in bad shape."

Michael weaved on his feet, but he had the strength to lift his finger and point it at the sheriff. "There's something I haven't said yet, but you had better understand. If you don't seek justice in this matter, Joaquín will. He'll become the judge, the jury *and* the executioner. And, Sheriff, a rope or a bullet would be a blessing to any one of those men before Joaquín is finished."

"If he kills men, he'll sure enough hang himself!" the sheriff snapped. "Ain't no greasers going to take justice into their own hands."

"There is no justice in California!" Michael cried, staggering toward the door.

Thirteen

MICHAEL REMEMBERED striking out on foot for Agua Fria in the hope of finding Joaquín before he went on his vengeance trail, but that was all he remembered until he woke in a room beside whose lone window stood Señorita Aurora López.

Michael was lying flat on his back with a turban-like bandage wound tightly around his head. As before, his vision swam and he saw double until he squeezed his eyes shut and Aurora appeared in sharp focus. She looked older than he remembered. The light was poor and her face was cast in shadow, but he could see that her cheeks were glistening with tears.

Thunder rolled, terminating with a sodden bang. A blast of wind shook the walls as hard sheets of rain pelted the windowpane with the same hurricane force Michael remembered at Cape Horn when the *Orion* had floundered and almost sank. A sharp crack of thunder brought Michael straight up in his bed.

Aurora turned suddenly and rushed to his side and pushed him back down flat. "Señor Callahan, the doctor said that you should not sit up so soon!"

"Where am I?"

"We are in Sonora."

"Sonora? But how . . ."

"You were delirious when I found you in Stockton. Since you

had no money or friends except for our people, we brought you here where you will be safe until you recover."

Michael closed his eyes and it brought all the memories rushing back to him again.

"Señorita," he whispered, "I owe you my apologies. I was—"

"Shhh!" Aurora placed a finger over his lips. "I know what you were going to say, and it is not necessary. It was . . . when I think of it, even flattering."

"Flattering?"

"Yes. That you should be so hurt at the thought that Joaquín and I were still lovers."

"I'm an idiot."

"You are badly hurt."

"Joaquín will kill the men who killed his wife." Michael sighed with resignation. "And then he will be hunted down like a rabid dog and shot or hanged. You must help me to find him, Aurora. Find him before he begins to kill them one by one."

"It is too late," she said. "Joaquín has already killed two."

"When!"

"He found them in Angel's Camp two days ago. They were in a saloon, and when they came out he was on his stallion again, swinging the same reata they used against his back."

Michael did not really want to hear the rest of the story, but he could not bring himself to silence the woman.

"They say that he roped one around the neck and spurred his stallion up the street. It was raining and the man's head was driven through the mud until he choked to death."

"The second man, what did he do?"

"He tried to kill Joaquín with his gun, but he was too drunk. Joaquín shot him—between his legs."

Aurora bent her head and made the sign of the cross before continuing. "They say the man died very badly and very slow."

"And I suppose that everyone in the camp was watching?"

Aurora nodded her head.

"What were the names of the men Joaquín killed?"

Aurora thought about that for a moment. "Señors Snyder and Blackman."

"That leaves Bates, Rawlings and . . . and a third man whose name is . . . Moore."

"Maybe they will leave California to save their lives."

"Maybe, but I doubt it. Either way, however, Joaquín is now a hunted man—a killer on the run."

Aurora raised her head suddenly. "They will *not* catch him! They will never catch him."

"Yes, they will," Michael said. "Sooner or later they'll catch and hang him and anyone that rides at his side."

Michael reached out and took Aurora's hands. "We have to convince him to leave California."

"He will never do that."

"He *must,* or he is a dead man."

Fresh tears rolled down Aurora's cheeks, and she produced a lace handkerchief to dry them.

"Are you still so much in love with him?"

Aurora López stood up and moved back to the window, where she watched the rain pouring down outside. For a long time she said nothing.

"Aurora, I need to know."

She turned. "I do not know myself anymore, Michael. I am . . . am very confused. My head and my heart tell me different things."

"What does your heart tell you?"

She sniffled again. "You would like better what my head is saying."

Michael tried to hide his severe disappointment by saying, "Your head is telling you the same thing I just told you—that Joaquín has no chance if he remains in California. But your heart, now that is telling you that he will live forever, untamed, and that you will be his new woman and he will love you always."

A sob escaped Aurora's red lips and she bent forward and covered her face to weep. Michael climbed slowly out of bed and padded over to her side. He put his arm around her shoulders, drawing her to his chest.

"Your heart is your betrayer, just as mine has been. But your heart can change, Aurora. It can and it will change, if I have anything to say about it."

She stopped weeping and looked up at him. "We must save Joaquín before he is killed."

"Only a bullet or a rope will stop him before he has avenged Rosita."

She drew away for a moment, staring up into his face, her eyes begging. "But we can try! We can try, Michael."

"Yes," he said, cradling her head back to his chest. "We can and we will try. But I have no money even for an old horse. Every cent I owned was either stolen or burned to ash."

"My father was not as poor as he seemed, Michael. I have the money for important things. And finding Joaquín is very important."

Michael agreed, despite knowing that Aurora's reasons for wanting to find the outlaw vaquero would break his heart.

"I'll be well enough to travel by tomorrow," he told her.

"No, the doctor says at least one week."

"Three days. Not one day more."

Aurora nodded, because she knew as well as Michael that, with every passing day, the odds were that either Joaquín or another one of Rosita's murderers was going to die.

IT WAS A COLD DECEMBER AFTERNOON when they rode through the muddy streets of Sawmill Flat to find the town in an uproar.

"What's going on?" Michael inquired from atop a stout bay mare that Aurora had purchased for him in Sonora before leaving.

"There's been a hanging!" a prospector said. "And someone flogged the dead body with a whip while it was dancin' in the air."

Aurora paled, gripping her saddle horn. Michael saw the big

crowd up ahead and pulled back his horse. "Aurora, you'd better stay here while I go on up and investigate."

"It was that damned greaser again!" the same prospector shouted. "His name is Joaquín Murieta."

"How can you be sure?"

"Because Jess Lawson saw the spectacle last night about eleven o'clock! Saw it with his own eyes."

"And he didn't raise the alarm?"

"He was drunk, and Joaquín said that if he got up from the ground he'd be whipped and hanged too!"

The prospector pointed a finger at Aurora. "Say, you're a damned Mexican!"

"Aurora, you'd better go back up the road and wait in the trees. This could get ugly."

Already it was getting ugly. Several men, attracted by the loud shouting of the prospector, glanced over to see Michael and Aurora. One of them cursed and started forward and the rest fell in behind.

"Hey, mister, I recognize you!" the leader challenged. "You're that damned greaser-lover they call the Gringo Amigo!"

"Go on!" Michael shouted at Aurora.

"Not without you."

"Grab her horse!"

Michael yanked his six-gun from his holster and aimed it at the leader's bearded face. "One more step and, mister, you're a dead man."

They froze.

"You're in cahoots with that Murieta fella, ain't you!" the man demanded.

"No! But whoever he whipped and hanged deserved to die."

"Moore was a hard man, but only a demon would flog a man at the same time he was strangling at the end of a bloody reata."

A shiver passed through Michael. "A bloody reata?"

"That's right!"

Michael didn't need to see the reata to know it was the same one that had been used to slice apart Joaquín's own back. And though he had no way of being sure, he was fairly certain that Moore had probably been the man who had done the flogging.

"Let's go, Aurora. Turn around and ride."

"We'll get you too, *Amigo,*" the leader said with contempt. "And the fact that she's a woman ain't gonna save her brown hide."

"I know that, señor," Aurora spat. "It did not save Rosita. Only I will kill the first gringo who touches me."

Michael read the pure hatred in their faces, and he knew that he and Aurora had to leave now before the crowd realized what was going on and came to tear them from their horses, drawn guns or no drawn guns.

"Let's go!" he shouted.

Aurora did not need further urging. She turned her own bay horse and spurred away. She was an expert horsewoman and Michael had no fear of being overtaken.

"If you choose to help Murieta, we'll get you, greaser-lover!"

Michael backed his horse into the trees, sawed hard on the reins and plunged through the forest.

IN THE COLD, DREARY WEEKS that followed, Michael and Aurora scoured the entire southern gold fields as far south as Mariposa and as far north as Grass Valley, always hearing Joaquín's name but never finding him. Joaquín Murieta was becoming a symbol of resistance among the thousands of angry Mexicans who refused to be driven out of California. To them Joaquín was a great man who dared to fight back. Among the whites and Chinese, however, Joaquín was hated and beginning to be feared.

In San Andreas, Michael and Aurora read that Joaquín and several of his growing band had robbed and murdered six Chinamen for their gold—which one tearful survivor of the Chinese camp claimed was worth more than twenty thousand dollars. Similar attacks, robberies and murders by Joaquín against the largely defenseless Chinese were also recounted.

"Joaquín would never do that!" Michael said, hurling the paper into the street with anger.

"Of course not," Aurora said, picking up the paper and reading the accounts for herself. "What is happening is that Joaquín has become the scapegoat for every crime that remains unsolved. Either that, or there are other banditos claiming to be Joaquín and using his name for their own protection."

"We've just got to find him."

LATE IN DECEMBER, Michael and Aurora arrived in Mokelumne Hill. Rain and sleet made travel almost impossible and they were forced to board their horses and look for a room in one of the local hotels. The Mok Hill Hotel was hard-used but clean. Michael paid for two rooms. As he was standing in the lobby, he asked an old man seated on one of the threadbare sofas if he had heard of Joaquín.

"Who hasn't!" the old man exclaimed. "He and his boys just murdered two men and hung them off a bridge a couple miles south of town. Shot the hell out of 'em first."

"What were their names?"

"Bill Rawlings and Eddie Bates," the old man said. "They were a couple of outlaws themselves, but they were white men."

Michael glanced across the room to see if the señorita had heard this news. He could tell by her paleness that she had overheard every single word.

"How can you be sure it was Murieta?" he asked, knowing full well that it was Joaquín, who had at last satisfied his revenge.

"Oh, it was Joaquín Murieta all right! He was seen the very night it happened in the Gold Pan Saloon down the street. I guess he had a few of his friends and they ran everyone in the place out and took it over for themselves. I heard them shooting out the chandeliers. They got roaring drunk and went riding out of town about midnight. Poor Rawlings and Bates weren't found until the next morning at daybreak. By then, those bloody greasers were long gone."

"If it makes any difference," Michael said, "Joaquín was avenging the murder of his young wife."

The old man didn't bat an eye at this bit of news. "Don't make any difference to me. All I know is that folks are pretty upset about Murieta. I hear tell that he's forming quite a band of cutthroats and starting to raid, murder and rob all over the state."

"That's ridiculous!" Aurora protested, coming over to join them.

"Why? He's wanted for murdering dozens of men already. So what does Joaquín and those that ride with him have to lose?"

Michael could see the logic. He could also see that it was useless to defend Joaquín. No doubt he had indeed shot and hanged Rawlings and Bates. And whether or not he'd killed all the other victims that were now being accounted to him and his gang was a pointless issue. The truth of the matter was that Joaquín was going to hang if he were captured.

Michael took Aurora's arm. "I'll take you upstairs to your room," he said. "You look exhausted."

Aurora gave him her arm and several of the other hotel guests stared with unconcealed envy as Michael led the beautiful señorita toward the staircase. Even dirty, tired and smelling of leather and horse, Aurora was the kind of woman who attracted attention.

Michael halted at the base of the stairs and called back to the hotel clerk. "Please have someone bring the lady up a bath right away."

The old hotel clerk nodded wearily and clapped his hands. A moment later, two Chinese children who could not have been more than ten years old came scurrying inside to take the saddlebags and show the new guests to their second-floor rooms. Michael tipped them a dime each and sent them back down the stairs.

"Bathe, take a nap and I'll come by at dusk and we'll find us something to eat," he said.

But Aurora hesitated beside the door. "What can we do

now?" she asked in a voice leadened with defeat. "We can't save Joaquín. It's too late."

Michael leaned heavily against the doorjamb. "I don't know," he admitted.

"Do you know what day this is?"

"No."

"December twenty-fourth. Tomorrow is Christmas."

"Christmas. I've missed the last several entirely."

"I saw a little adobe chapel out at the edge of town. You might be the only gringo at midnight Mass, but will you come with me? I think we need God's help and blessing. I *know* that Joaquín needs our prayers."

"All right," Michael said. "I guess so."

That night was one that Michael would not soon forget. The congregation was entirely Mexican, but the Mass was spoken in Latin and he could follow it easily because of his own Catholic upbringing. For the first time in a long, long while, Michael found himself remembering his childhood. His father had been a hod carrier who was chronically out of work because of the drink. His mother was long-suffering, deeply religious and un-wavering in her faith. She bore six children—three raised to adulthood, three never living past the age of ten.

Michael remembered his childhood as being mostly heartache and poverty, with little joy or beauty except for the lovely church and the intensely satisfying Mass. During his teenage years he had found comfort in prayer for the simple reason that it was all that there was of hope.

His father drank himself to death in 1843 and, to the surprise of no one except the Callahan family itself, life improved. When Michael boarded the *Orion,* his mother had told him not to write —just to come home again when the gold rush was over. Rich or poor, she'd said, he should come home with his head held high.

At the Christmas Eve Mass, Aurora linked her arm through Michael's. He was easily the tallest man in the church and, being the only Caucasian earned more than a few hard stares, which he did not even notice.

Michael, immersed in the few good memories of his youth, lulled by the soft rhythmic Latin and at peace with himself on this rare occasion, was deeply grateful that he had attended Mass with Aurora. He realized that time and gold fever had eroded away all but the bedrock core of his spirituality.

Afterward, in a crowded little hall attached to the chapel, they stayed to eat some sweet breads and Mexican candies and drink strong black coffee. Michael, aware that some did not approve of him, said little, but Aurora, with her charm and beauty, managed to attract quite a crowd and quickly dispelled any potential hostility when she introduced Michael as the Gringo Amigo. When the people heard this, Michael became a celebrity. Food—too much of it—was foisted upon him. A few Mexicans had guitars and the rest sang Christmas hymns in their native tongue. Michael had never heard these songs before, but he would not soon forget them. Children yawned, quarreled and fell asleep in their mothers' arms. A few clutched small, handmade Christmas presents.

When the hour grew very late, Michael and Aurora wished everyone a joyous season, then ducked outside into a cold rain. They hurried back toward their hotel, with Michael holding a coat over Aurora's head to shield her.

"That was beautiful," he said. "I would never have done it without your urging."

"I have a confession of my own," she said. "I would not have gone without you."

Under the shelter of a storefront porch, Michael stopped Aurora and blurted, "I would like to take you again next Christmas Eve. And all the remaining Christmas Eves of my life."

Aurora's smile faded. "Please, you must not think like that."

"I can't help it."

He felt so helpless and pathetic that it must have shown, because Aurora raised up on her tiptoes and kissed him full on the lips. It wasn't just a quick peck, either. But before Michael could crush her to his body, Aurora slipped away and was walking down the muddy street.

He hurried after her, caught her and took her arm. "I want to buy you something for Christmas, but I have no money."

"Then you may use some of mine."

"What kind of idea is that?"

"I don't mind," she said, with a lilt in her voice.

Michael grinned and, despite the foul weather, they walked the rest of the way to the hotel in a good, happy silence. He was falling in love again, even though that surely made him California's biggest fool, since he was certain that Aurora still loved Joaquín. But down deep inside, Michael knew that she would love him one day.

Michael stood dripping in the hallway outside of Aurora's door. "Good night, querida."

She swallowed. "Buenos noches."

Michael's hands came up to hold her, but she stepped back and gently, firmly closed the door.

For a long while, Michael stood pressed against her door, needing only to hear the sound of her movement. Finally he went to his own room. For some reason, and despite all logic— for she had given him no hope—he felt ecstatic. During what little time remained of the night, Michael found it in him to write a love letter.

December 25, 1852

My Beloved Aurora:

In Latin, your beautiful name means the "dawn." And like the Christmas dawn I now see outside, you bring the fresh hope of a new beginning. Each day that we have spent together, you have brought me joy where before there was only sorrow. During these past few months, I have found myself feeling guilty because of my inner happiness and the fact that we have not found Joaquín and the news of him has always been bad.

After Tessa, I thought my heart was too shattered ever to be made whole again. But I was wrong. I wish I were of your

race but, failing that, at least I am of your religion and in kin
with your spirit. Much more, I think, than is Joaquín. I do not
wish his death—God knows that I do not. I want him to
simply disappear. To return to Sonora and use his plunder to
buy a huge ranch and to pay penances to God for delivering
him from an early grave. I want him to ride his horses and be
a vaquero again, strong, happy and proud. To make his
rawhide ropes and show the young boys how to do it
properly, always in winter, always at the time of a full moon.

I want Joaquín to marry another beautiful Mexican girl like
Rosita who can heal the pain, the hatred and the bitterness in
his heart. I want him to grow old and watch his sons and
daughters walk in circles around a sleepy little Mexican plaza,
exchanging shy glances and spring flowers. I want him to see
his children become tall and wise and have children of their
own as he grows old with dignity.

I want long life for Joaquín Murieta—but I want Aurora
López for myself. Is this so wrong? Am I due so little love and
happiness of my own, dear Lord? Surely this is not too much
to ask.

Dear Aurora, if I could, I would buy you the moon and the
stars for Christmas presents this day. Instead, I give you my
heart.

> Your devoted friend,
> MICHAEL W. CALLAHAN, Esq.

Fourteen

MICHAEL AND AURORA had returned to winter in Hornitos, where they had many friends and where they were sure that Joaquín would find them. With each passing day, more and more murders, robberies and vicious attacks were attributed to Joaquín and his band of cutthroats.

Michael and Aurora subscribed to all the little gold field newspapers, as well as the big city ones like San Francisco's *Alta California*, the Sacramento *Union*, the Los Angeles *Star* and Stockton's San Joaquin *Republican*. Not an issue arrived that did not recount, often in lurid detail, the crimes of Joaquín Murieta and his bloodthirsty gang.

"Listen to this one," Michael said one February afternoon as he and Aurora were leaving the little store where mail was collected. "It's from a newspaper correspondent in Mokelumne Hill. 'Not less than twenty innocent persons have been murdered in this vicinity within a month and robbery is an everyday occurrence, thanks to Joaquín Murieta and his blood-lusting desperados.'"

Michael shook his head and selected another paper. "Or this high-sounding tripe in the Jackson newspaper: 'The singular success of Joaquín in his daring and numberless robberies, and still more in his numerous hairbreadth escapes, is something unparalleled in history. He is now the terror of the whole country, and no man is safe who travels alone. It is reputed that Joaquín has many bands of Mexican desperados all over the gold country. Horse thieving—but only for the highest quality to be found—is even more important to these ruthless banditos than gold. For gold alone cannot keep them out of the clutches of the law, not like the speed and endurance of superior horseflesh.' "

Aurora stopped and turned to Michael. "Why doesn't Joaquín explain all this to us?"

"I don't know," Michael confessed, for he had often asked himself the same question. "Perhaps Joaquín simply wants to shield us from any association with himself."

"That is a matter that *we* should decide," Aurora said. "We hear of him stealing horses in the Central Valley, robbing and murdering in Los Angeles, even capturing a paddle-wheel steamer on the Sacramento River and executing passengers for their valuables. I don't know what to believe anymore."

"I keep tracking all the crimes and writing letters to the newspapers," Michael said. "I am doing all I can to tell the people that Joaquín cannot possibly be committing those bloody outrages. That he is a decent man and that, from what we can determine, every two-bit bandito in California is starting to call himself Joaquín."

"But it's not helping!" Aurora lamented. "Michael, I'm sorry, but the gringos want to blame everything on our Joaquín, and at the same time the Mexicans believe he is a great hero. They call him the 'Ghost of Sonora' or 'El Patrio'—the Patriot. It is crazy."

"Only Joaquín himself can tell us the truth."

Aurora sighed. "But would he? And what if he did commit those terrible murders?"

"The only ones Joaquín killed were those who deserved to die."

Aurora made the sign of the cross. "So much hatred and blood," she whispered. "So much death!"

Michael put his arm around the senorita's shoulders. "I don't think we can believe anything we hear or read about Joaquín. We must wait to hear the truth from Joaquín Murieta himself."

"I am afraid that we will never see him alive again."

Aurora folded against Michael's chest and Michael comforted her. The perfume of her lustrous black hair made his senses reel. He was sure that she was at last falling in love with him and that, inevitably, they would be wed. Toward this end, he had been escorting Aurora to the little adobe church in Hornitos every Sunday. Now they were already an integral part of the congregation and Michael was a respected parishioner. Before the end of summer, Michael was certain that Father Antonio Mendoza would perform the sacrament of marriage before his beautiful little altar.

But that evening Michael's world was shaken to its very foundation. A hush fell over the small cafe where he and Aurora were eating as Joaquín stepped inside.

"Joaquín!" Michael exclaimed, coming to his feet.

Aurora, whose back was to the front door, twisted around and a look of great joy came over her face. She knocked her chair over as she ran across the room to throw herself in Joaquín's arms.

The smile died on Michael's lips as Joaquín embraced the woman he loved. "Señor," he managed to say, "it is good to see you again."

"And you, Amigo," Joaquín said before he turned to the doorway and told about a half dozen of his gang to ride on to the cantina before he led Aurora back to their table.

The patrons of the cafe, perhaps a dozen, had forgotten the food on their plates and the cerveza in their glasses as they stared reverently at Joaquín. A small boy of about six broke away from his family and rushed to the vaquero's side to hug his fancy, bell-bottomed leather pants.

Joaquín, black eyes twinkling, disengaged himself from Aurora, reached into his soft leather vest and presented the boy with a gold nugget. When the child's eyes grew round, everyone in the room laughed. Joaquín reached back into his vest and amazed everyone by producing a handful of small gold nuggets. He then told the people to step outside and he would give them a little "gold rush" all their own. A moment later he hurled the nuggets into the street, hooked his thumbs into his fancy gunbelt and laughed loudly to see the people scramble in the street like chickens after tossed corn.

For the first time, Michael realized that Joaquín had not dismissed all of his men to the nearby cantina. A large and brutish fellow, who wore crossed bandoliers on his massive chest, remained. Two six-guns were strapped around his thick waist, and he held a double-barreled shotgun in his meaty fists. Michael's eyes widened when he noticed that this man had lost the index finger on his right hand. This had to be the terrible "Three-fingered Jack." His real name was Manuel García. Some newspaper accounts claimed that García had lost his finger while dallying his reata. Others swore the finger had been shot off during the Mexican War. The only thing that everyone did agree on was that Three-fingered Jack was a vicious murderer.

Seeing Michael stare contemptuously at his bodyguard, Joaquín ordered Three-fingered Jack to wait just outside.

"Tequila!" Joaquín ordered. Then with Aurora's waist still encircled by his hand, he said, "My good and faithful friends, we have much to talk about."

But no one said a word until a bottle was brought to their table and Joaquín had finished rolling a cigarette.

Michael studied Joaquín. He had changed in manner and also in appearance. No longer was he thin and hungry-looking, and now there was a steely hardness in his restless eyes.

"Why didn't you come sooner?" Michael asked.

"Because our friendship could bring you trouble."

"They're saying you are a cold-blooded killer," Aurora blurted. "Every day we read terrible stories about you and your gang."

"You can read anything, but that does not mean that it is true."

"That's why Michael has been writing to the newspapers, telling them that you could not possibly do the terrible things they say."

Joaquín leaned back in his chair. He took a long drink, puckered his lips and dropped the front legs down on the floor with such a loud noise that Three-fingered Jack jumped back inside with his shotgun up and ready to fire.

"It is all right," Joaquín shouted at his startled guard. "Come have a drink with us!"

García was only too happy to follow this order. He took Michael's own water glass, filled it with tequila, raised it in a mock salute, then drank and marched outside to close the door.

"García," Joaquín said, lowering his voice to a confidential whisper, "is a very dangerous hombre. He hates the Chinese even worse than the gringos."

"Is he the one who is slitting their throats in the camps?" Michael asked.

Joaquín rolled his eyes crazily and made a circling motion with his forefinger. "Manuel sometimes goes a little loco. Comprende?"

"I'm afraid I do."

Aurora reached for the bottle, poured herself a stiff drink and tossed it down straight. She was very pale when she said, "How much of what we read is true, Joaquín?"

The vaquero shrugged. "I have men and they kill. As for myself, I kill only when it is absolutely necessary. And never in anger."

"They say you steal many horses," Michael said. "Only the best."

"That is the only truth I have read. But I take only what is needed to keep us alive. And when I need fresh ones, I give the tired ones to our poor people. Is that so wrong?"

"It is in the eyes of the law."

"You must stop the killing," Aurora pleaded. "You must leave California and go to Mexico."

Joaquín emptied his glass. "If I did this, would you come with me?"

Michael's breath caught in his throat. He was sure that he knew Aurora's answer. It seemed like forever before she answered.

"No," she said, reaching out to take Michael's hand and squeeze it tightly. "I would stay here with the Gringo Amigo."

Michael breathed again. His heart jumped in his chest and, in a daze, he reached for the bottle, then drank straight from it.

"You have changed much," Joaquín said to Aurora, his eyes tightening at the corners, as he peered through the smoke of his cigarette. "But even if I have lost your love, I have at least given our people a reason to hold their heads high again."

"Your hands are stained with blood," Aurora whispered.

"This *land* is stained with Mexican blood!"

"Don't shout at her," Michael said in a tight voice. "She still loves us both."

Joaquín stiffened and his eyes sparkled. The thought occurred to Michael that he might be very close to death, but suddenly Joaquín relaxed.

"My friends," Joaquín said, tossing down more tequila, "did you know the gringos hanged Reyes Feliz in San Gabriel?"

"No," Aurora said in a barely audible voice. "When?"

"Last November," Joaquín choked. "They strung him up along with Cipriano Sandoval and Benito López. Reyes was like a brother to me. He was only nineteen."

"But why?"

"Does it matter?"

Michael and Aurora exchanged glances. Joaquín was so filled with anger and hatred he seemed as fragile inside as fine crystal.

"I wish we could help you," Michael said.

"Maybe you can."

"How?"

Joaquín glanced over his shoulder to make certain Three-fingered Jack could not hear what he was about to reveal. "I am weary of this life. I have no love for killing, and a man can take only so much running and looking over his shoulder. Now they are considering a big reward for my head."

Aurora gasped at this news. Michael said, "Do you fear this reward?"

"I fear nothing," Joaquín answered, without any emotion. "But if the money is big, then, sooner or later, someone will betray me."

"I still don't see how we can help."

"Have you heard of a man named Joaquín Valenzuela?"

"Yes, he is said to be a cold-blooded murderer."

"This is true, Amigo. Like my compadre outside the door, he likes to kill those who cannot defend themselves. And that is why I have a plan."

"A plan?"

"Sí. One that might save my life and make you good money. If it fails, we might all end up with our throats cut." To emphasize that, he made a hacking motion with his index finger.

Aurora took another drink of tequila. "Tell us your plan, Joaquín. If it is not against the laws of God, then I will help."

"Same here," Michael vowed.

Joaquín chuckled. " 'Against the laws of God'? I have not heard anyone consider His wishes in a long, long time, señorita. It is good to be reminded."

The vaquero dropped his cigarette to the floor and ground it out with the heel of his boot. Before speaking, Joaquín refilled their glasses, then called for another bottle of tequila. When it was before him, and the three of them were again alone, Joaquín leaned forward and hurriedly whispered his plan.

Fifteen

MICHAEL did not see Joaquín again soon, but he knew he would by summer. In the meantime he kept detailed notes and made daily entries in his third diary. Many of his notes were simply observations about the gold rush itself. Michael wrote that, in the fifth year since John Marshal had discovered gold at Sutter's Mill, the production of placer gold sharply declined. To make up for this, the rugged, independent prospector was being replaced by machinery. The most profitable mining was now being done by large companies that could afford the kind of heavy equipment and steam engines necessary to bore great holes in the mountains in order to track veins of gold. The most disturbing new introduction was hydraulic mining. In this practice an incredible amount of water pressure was generated by diverting a good-sized stream into a long wooden flume that fed into a huge, openmouthed pipe standing vertical against a cliff. The entire stream was then funneled down into a small-diameter hose and nozzle. Michael was awed by the sight of the water blasting away an entire mountainside. An oozing sea of mud and rubble was created, enabling an army of miners to slog about in the muck seeking gold.

"This is the most damnable thing I've seen introduced in the gold fields yet," Michael said while watching a giant pine being ripped off the side of a mountain to be swallowed in the mud.

"Look at what it's doing to the land! It will silt and clog up the rivers feeding down to the Central Valley. Just wait until the farmers downriver see all the brown water come rushing through their agricultural communities."

Aurora agreed.

The day after witnessing the carnage of hydraulic mining, Michael wrote a newspaper account describing it in detail. He sent it off to the newspaper in Jackson, along with another defense of Joaquín Murieta. He received five dollars for his story on hydraulic mining, but the editor did not dare print his defense of the West's most infamous bandito. Public sentiment against Joaquín was reaching the threshold of hysteria.

On February 8 the *Columbia Gazette* said that six Chinese miners were slaughtered on the Big Bar of the Cosumnes River, reportedly losing six thousand dollars to Joaquín and his band. Only a few days later the *San Joaquin Republican* printed the following: "The reward of one thousand dollars offered by the governor for the capture of Joaquín . . . is deemed entirely inadequate to the importance and expense of his arrest and cast a gloom over this ill-fated country. Already the citizens of this country have raised and expended more than that amount to stay the murderous band but it is not yet done and it is clearly proved that Joaquín won't be taken by ordinary means."

Just three days later, that same newspaper reported under bold headlines that Joaquín Murieta and his band had robbed the stage that ran between Sacramento and Mokelumne Hill, killing the driver and two women passengers. Posses on horseback and afoot patrolled the roads while others ransacked the Mexican communities in a fit of desperation and revenge. No young adult Mexican was safe if he were caught alone on horseback.

The *Sacramento Union* reported: "This town is under the greatest excitement. A large meeting of the citizens was held this evening and severe measures were taken that must eventually lead to the capture of the murderers. Nearly the whole population has volunteered to turn out in the pursuit tomorrow. One thousand dollars are offered for the head of Joaquín. His band is supposed to number over fifty men scattered over the country."

At almost the same time this news appeared, Joaquín himself rode into Hornitos with Three-fingered Jack and four of his band. They arrived at night and sent for Michael.

The moon was full. Michael could see the Mexicans and their fine horses were thin and hard-used. Joaquín dismounted and, as he approached, Michael noted that he was limping badly and that his shoulders were slumped with weariness. Joaquín took Michael by the arm and led him out of earshot.

"It is time to spring our little trap," he said. "You must go to Sacramento tomorrow and do your part."

"I will try," Michael vowed. "I can only try."

"I know," Joaquín said, glancing over his shoulder. "I will contact you when the hounds are near the fox. Eh?"

Michael nodded. No one had to tell him what would happen to either of them if Three-fingered Jack, Joaquín Valenzuela or any of the other most desperate banditos even suspected this plot.

Joaquín started to turn away, then said, "If anything goes wrong, I cannot save you or the señorita."

"I know that."

"You would have to run for your lives."

"I know that too." Michael placed his hand on Joaquín's shoulder. "But this is going to work."

"Sí," Joaquín said, without much hope in his voice. And then he said something that really struck Michael hard. "Adios, my Gringo Amigo."

Michael's throat constricted so suddenly that he could only nod his head as his friend limped back to the others and mounted his horse. Joaquín was no longer riding the gray stallion. Michael remembered that fine animal had been shot out from under him in a gun battle near San Andreas. Maybe the dead or dying horse had fallen on Joaquín's leg, causing the limp.

When Joaquín and his grim banditos galloped away in the

darkness, Michael returned to his room. He was far too agitated to sleep, so, since it was only two hours before daybreak, he sat down at his writing desk and opened his diary. He began to write.

May 19, 1853

Aurora and I will depart for Sacramento this morning. It is our plan that I become one of the California Rangers specifically hired to chase down and kill Joaquín Murieta and his bandit gang. I believe I will be successful in obtaining this commission because of my friend Paddy Ryan's great influence with Governor Bigler. Also, I can post evidence that I am on familiar terms with Joaquín and, therefore, can greatly aid in his capture.

Should I fail to obtain this commission, I will somehow ingratiate myself to whomever is designated to be in command of the new California Ranger force and offer my services gratis. I am sure that they will be accepted because few whites have ever seen the real face of Joaquín Murieta.

Aurora López has agreed to marry me when this crisis has passed. Either here or in some faraway place if that becomes necessary in order to save our lives. I am supremely happy. Happier than I ever dreamed I could be and very confident that all will turn out right. God is on our side and in our daily prayers. And with His blessing I will one day visit New York to show my mother my new bride.

TWO DAYS LATER they rode wearily into Sacramento and went straight to Paddy's Emporium. After hurried introductions the three of them went into his office where Michael closed and locked the door.

"What the hell is this all about?" Paddy exclaimed. "Are you and Miss López in trouble?"

"No," Michael said, "but we need some help."

Quickly Michael explained Joaquín's plan.

"You're out of your mind!" Paddy exclaimed. "Captain Harry Love has been put in command of a force of twenty California Rangers. He's a killer himself and he won't brook any shenanigans."

"I must find this fellow immediately," Michael said. "I want to become one of these Rangers."

"Impossible!" Paddy turned to Aurora. "Señorita," he pleaded, "talk some sense into him! He's no manhunter. He'll just get himself killed. I don't know what he's up to or what has possessed his reason, but this is madness."

"You must trust him," Aurora said quietly.

"Trust him?" Paddy's face reddened. "Why, I'd trust him with my life or even my money, but I can't in good conscience allow him to go riding off on a dangerous manhunt. Joaquín Murieta and his band are desperate men. They will not be taken alive."

"Where can I find this Harry Love?" Michael asked impatiently.

"At the Delta Saloon, most likely," Paddy finally said with resignation. "You won't like him. He's a big Texan, loud, profane and ill-mannered. They say he is brave, and I do not doubt it for a minute, but I would not want him to be behind me if I had so much as a dollar in my pocket."

"I understand."

Michael handed his old friend a leather satchel.

"What's this for?"

"Put it in your office safe and keep it for me until I return."

"Is it money? Did you *finally* make some real money?"

Paddy looked so pleased and excited that Michael did not have the heart to tell him the truth. "Yes."

"Hot damn!" Paddy cried. "What'd you do, make a big strike?"

"That's right."

"How much? Where?"

"Not now," Michael said. "I'll tell you all about it later."

Paddy suddenly grew cautious. "Well, why don't you deposit

this in our bank. We can go over there tomorrow and open an account. It'd be safer in a bank, Mike."

"I want you to keep it," Michael said. "I might need it in a hurry sometime."

Paddy frowned. He examined his old friend very closely. "Are you sure you didn't get kicked in the head or something? You're not making much sense to me."

"I will, later. Just trust me. For old times' sake."

"All right," Paddy said. "Now, tonight you and Miss López are going to be our guests for dinner. And believe you me, we'll do it up right. This time, *I* pay. You paid last time."

"Fair enough."

"Good! You've both got a lot of explaining to do, but it can wait until after dinner, over brandy and one of my cigars."

"Okay." Michael took Aurora's arm. "Beautiful, isn't she?"

"Yes," Paddy said, meaning it. "It appears to me that your luck has finally turned to the good."

"It was about time, don't you think?"

"I sure do." Paddy almost bounced up and down with happiness. "I can't wait to tell Pearl about this."

Michael started out the door. "Oh, Paddy?"

"Yeah."

"Here," Michael said, reaching into his coat pocket and pulling out the article on hydraulic mining that he had written with such passion. "Read this and make it your issue. You'll be a hero, and it will propel you right into the political arena, where you belong."

"This is the best store in Sacramento!" Paddy said with a tone of indignation.

"I know, I know. I used to run it, remember? But as good a merchant as you are, you're needed in politics, and this hydraulic mining thing is your ticket."

"I've heard about it," Paddy said, trying to tear his eyes from the article.

"You need to become the expert on it," Michael said, "and that will give you a fair start."

Michael escorted Aurora out the door.

"Where are we going now?"

"You're going to your hotel room. I'm going to find Captain Love and sign on as one of his Rangers."

"Oh, no," she said. "I'm going with you."

"But you heard what Paddy said about this man. He's not the kind I want you to meet."

"You might be surprised how easily handled that kind of man can be if a woman uses her wits."

Michael scowled. He didn't like the idea of Aurora accompanying him to the Delta Saloon one darn bit, but then he wasn't in any position to tell her what to do or what not to do, so they marched out of the Emporium and headed down the street.

Sixteen

THE DELTA SALOON was located near the riverfront, and it was not the kind of establishment to which Michael would ever have taken a lady. The moment they entered, several dozen men turned to stare at Aurora. Michael went up to one of them.

"I need to see Captain Harry Love. Is he here tonight?"

The man, not taking his bold eyes off Aurora, gestured toward the bar. "Big fella with the big mouth."

"Come on," Michael said, taking Aurora's arm and leading her toward a cluster of men.

Aurora's presence stopped their conversation. As tall as Michael and a good fifty pounds heavier, Harry Love appeared to be in his mid-thirties and hard-used. He wore his hair shoulder-length, and it was tangled and dirty. With a three-day growth of beard, heavy beetle-like brows and a lantern jaw, Love gave Michael the impression of some kind of ape-man.

"What do you want?" Love demanded, his bloodshot eyes wandering from Michael to Aurora's bosom.

Michael stepped in front of Aurora, his every fiber revolted by the brutish manhunter. "We need to talk in private."

Angry that Michael had blocked his view of Aurora, Love started to shift sideways. Michael shifted as well, saying, "I can help you find Joaquín Murieta. He calls me the Gringo Amigo and he trusts me."

Now he had Love's complete attention. "What's she got to do with it?"

"She's his . . . his woman," Michael said, hating the lie but knowing it was necessary.

Love raised his eyebrows. "You know where Murieta is right now?"

"No. But I know where he'll be in the next few weeks. What's it worth to you?"

Love called for a fresh bottle of whiskey and three glasses. "Be back shortly, gents," he said to the men, as he scooped up his bottle and the glasses. Then he led Michael and Aurora over to a table where two men sat talking and drinking.

"Move!"

The pair not only moved, they jumped. "Sit," Love commanded.

Michael and Aurora sat, and when Love poured them drinks, they drank. Love refilled his own glass. "So," he said, "you're going to be Judas for a few pieces of silver."

"Gold," Aurora corrected, "and much more than a few pieces, señor."

"We'll see. Talk is cheap."

"We can deliver Joaquín," Michael stated.

"When?"

Michael shrugged. "Next time he comes around Hornitos. He's on the move a lot these days."

"He sure as hell is," Love said. "He and his murderin' greasers are riding their tails off trying to stay ahead of posses combing the hills from here to Mariposa and on over to the Pacific Coast."

"Joaquín is in Los Angeles," Aurora said. "You can search all you want in the gold country, but you won't find him there."

"Los Angeles?" Love scratched at the stubble of his beard. "I heard tell that he's hanging out around Mariposa."

"Not so," Michael said.

Love drank his whiskey. "How do I know that Joaquín didn't

send you up here to lead us around by the nose until we're all worn out?''

"What would that profit us?"

"You might owe him or he might have threatened to kill you if you didn't play a game on me and my Rangers," Love said bluntly.

Aurora shook her head. "We want five hundred dollars, señor. That's what it will cost if you want our help to find Joaquín Murieta before someone else claims the reward."

Love snickered and climbed to his feet. "Folks, I don't need your help *that* damn bad. We'll catch Joaquín, Three-fingered Jack and the whole bloody lot of them on our own hook."

"Why not do it the *easy* way, señor?" Aurora said with an inviting smile.

Love licked his lips. "Why don't you and I go off somewhere and talk about it together, señorita?"

Michael's cheeks flamed. Just as he was about to grab Love by the throat, Aurora said, "No thank you, señor. Perhaps some other time, when we can do business."

Love grinned wickedly. "Maybe I'll just keep that in mind if we have a little trouble trackin' down your man. But not for no five hundred dollars."

Aurora shrugged her shoulders as if it were of no importance. She gave Michael her hand and allowed herself to be escorted toward the front door.

Outside, Michael swallowed his anger. Aurora was just trying to draw Love into their trap, but even she had failed. "He didn't buy it."

"Perhaps they will change their minds when they discover that it is not so easy to catch Joaquín. Give them a little time. Right now, they have whiskey and everyone is looking up to them. They feel like big men."

Aurora took Michael's arm. "But in a month, maybe two, they will come to us."

"I hope you're right. And let's just hope that Captain Love isn't as good as he thinks he is."

"He's too big and heavy to catch the vaqueros."

Michael certainly hadn't thought of it like that. Captain Love was such a dominating physical presence that it was easy to see why he had convinced the California State Legislature that he was the only man qualified and capable of capturing Joaquín. But Aurora was correct—on the best day of his life, Harry Love could never have been a horseman equal to Joaquín Murieta.

"I guess, then, we return to Hornitos and wait," Michael said, without much enthusiasm.

Aurora stepped in front of him and wrapped her arms around his neck. "I was worried about you in there," she said. "I could feel your anger."

"Harry Love is a killer," Michael said tightly. "The only difference between him and a man like Three-fingered Jack is that he's got a badge to hide behind."

"It was more than that."

"Yeah," Michael admitted. "I hated the way he stared at you. It made me want to—"

Michael didn't finish because Aurora's lips silenced his angry words. He crushed her to his breast. When their lips finally parted, he pleaded, "Be my wife, Aurora. Marry me!"

"All right."

"You mean it?"

"Sí!"

Michael howled with joy. He had finally won something much more valuable than gold. "When, Aurora? I suppose that you will want to wait until after this is all over. That's all right with me, but—"

"No. I want to go back to Hornitos and have Father Mendoza marry us right away."

"I have to ask you this, and I will never ask it again. What about Joaquín?"

Aurora sighed. "I still admire him. He even fires my blood a little. But I don't love him anymore. I love *you.*"

Again, Michael crushed Aurora to his breast, and he thanked God for at last listening to his most fervent prayers.

. . . .

THEY WERE MARRIED in the little adobe chapel in Hornitos and the entire congregation celebrated their union. The Mass was simple, as was Aurora's wedding dress and the decorations, but the honest simplicity seemed to Michael to make the ceremony itself more special. When it was over, Michael and Aurora had a wonderful fiesta with guitars, singing and much feasting.

"Come," Aurora said, "I will teach you the contradanza."

"I'm not much of a dancer," Michael protested with more than a little apprehension.

But Aurora led him out on the dance floor anyway. Michael had seen the contradanza and knew that it was highly popular among the Mexican people. It was an intricate dance involving paired couples who stepped in unison. Each couple would line up and, as their turn arrived, would spin through the upraised arms of a second couple while the others clapped to a lively tempo.

"How about an Irish jig instead?" he asked nervously.

"You can teach me that when we go to see your mother in New York City," Aurora said with merriment in her dark eyes.

"Then a nice, slow waltz?"

"Come on," she said, pulling him into line as the music started and the gay couples began to clap their hands.

In a moment Michael was being propelled forward, and Aurora effortlessly guided him through all the steps. He felt clumsy as a loon, though no one noticed, and there was such happiness that soon he forgot his apprehension and was dancing with the best of them.

"You feel as light as a cloud in my arms," he told his new bride.

She kissed him and they whirled around and around. In the days and weeks to come, they shared their quiet honeymoon together in and around Hornitos waiting for the moment when they would be contacted by Captain Love and his Rangers. Michael was often to recall that dancing the contradanza with his new bride as the single happiest event of his life.

. . . .

FROM THE NEWSPAPERS Michael learned that Captain Love did not waste any time in setting about to capture Joaquín Murieta and any other Mexican banditos in the area. Michael thought it curious to read that the California legislation which created the Rangers said that the Rangers' purpose was to capture the "party or gang of robbers commanded by the five Joaquíns, whose names are Joaquín Muriati, Joaquín Ocomorenia, Joaquín Valenzuela, Joaquín Boteller, and Joaquín Carillo."

Michael showed this to Aurora, saying, "It proves what I've been writing for months now, that the Mexican name Joaquín is as common as the Anglo names William and John and that there are at least five Joaquíns that are raising hell in California."

"Yes," Aurora said, "but it's a poor editor who cannot even spell Murieta correctly. But he did spell Valenzuela right, didn't he?"

"Uh-huh," Michael said pensively. "He sure did."

According to the newspapers, Love wasted no time outfitting each of his twenty eager recruits with a pistol, rifle and bowie knife. They were also assigned the best horses money could buy, and Love made sure that they carried no extra baggage. Each man was allowed only the barest essentials, rolled up in an oilskin tarp.

On a hot day in June, Michael and Aurora watched the Rangers gallop through Hornitos to spend a few hours in the very cantina which Joaquín's own men favored. They also noted that, when the Rangers entered, the local Mexican populace was quick to disappear.

"They look tough and competent, don't they?" Michael observed.

Aurora nodded. "I would be lying if I told you that I wasn't afraid for Joaquín."

A week later, Captain Love and his California Rangers proved their worth by capturing a pair of Mexican horse thieves and thirty-one horses. The horses were delivered to their owners, but the rustlers were later found alongside the road, bodies riddled with bullets. In short order, other Mexicans, some only suspected thieves, either disappeared never to be seen again, or else were found hanged or shot.

So swift and merciless was Captain Love in his intent that, on July 6, the San Joaquin *Republican* happily proclaimed: "Robberies have ceased in Mariposa Co. The untiring effort of Capt. Love, Lieut. Connors and their brave company of Rangers have had the effect of completely ridding the country of the desperate murderers and horse-thieves who infest that county. The Rangers have been in the saddle nearly every day since they reached Mariposa Co.; they have recovered numerous bands of stolen horses and arrested many thieves . . . When they entered upon their duties, not a night passed that some house was not broken into, some animal stolen or some other robbery committed, while during the last three weeks not an act of the kind has been heard of. All honor then to Capt. Love's Rangers."

But by the terrible heat of mid-July the Rangers were beginning to become a nuisance, and there were rumors that they were demoralized. The wave of adulation and support they had first received had passed just as Aurora had predicted. The fact that they had yet to see, much less catch, Joaquín Murieta, played hard on their morale.

One day when the temperature was nearly one hundred degrees in the shade and the sun had burned the deep blue from the sky, Captain Love rode into Hornitos and found Michael at work building an adobe house for himself and his new wife. For several minutes the big Ranger captain sat on his thin, lathered horse and watched Michael make the adobe bricks while Aurora mixed the clay and straw and added the right amount of water.

"They add a little sand and horseshit to it down along the Rio Grande," Love said, "but the adobe still comes out the same. It's a damn sorry sight to see a white man and a beautiful woman doing the work of peons."

"It's honest work," Michael said, looking up. "About as hard as panning gold or working a sluice box."

Love couldn't take his eyes off Aurora in her bare feet and simple cotton dress.

"Make a pretty woman like you look old."

"I don't intend to do this the rest of my life, Señor Love."

Harry Love removed his wide-brimmed, sweat-stained hat. "Hotter than the hinges of hell," he observed. "Only thing that gives me any satisfaction these days is knowing that Murieta is suffering even worse. We've kept him running."

"Maybe."

Love climbed heavily down from his horse. He reached into his saddlebags and produced a bottle of warm whiskey, then uncorked it and took a long pull. He held it up to Michael and Aurora, who shook their heads.

"Suit yourselves." Love drank again, replaced the cork and walked a little unsteadily over to the water trough, where he let his horse drink. He removed his hat, filled it with water and jammed it back on his head, flooding himself liberally.

Sleeving his face, he turned and said, "I'm gettin' impatient and so are my men. You got some information, maybe we can make a deal."

"For five hundred dollars?" Michael asked.

"No. This is the deal. You tell me where I can catch Murieta and I'll make sure that neither of you wind up face down in a ditch and covered with flies."

Michael clenched his fists at his sides. Aurora was more vocal. "Do not threaten us, señor!"

"I'll do whatever it damn well takes to catch Murieta!" Love bellowed, advancing on them.

Michael was not wearing his sidearm, but he figured he was harder and quicker than Love. He might be able to whip the man with his fists, if he didn't get caught early with a haymaker.

"That's far enough."

Love stopped. His face was red and so were his eyes. Up close, he looked mean and even desperate. "I'll give you the same share of the thousand-dollar reward my men get if we kill Joaquín and his men."

"No," Michael said. "We want a hundred dollars . . . each."

"No deals," Love said. "I'll just see that you can afford the lumber to buy a decent house instead of that damn dirt one you're plannin'. That's it. I won't ask again. As long as Joaquín Murieta lives, the Mexican people have a symbol. Some of them are even talking about a revolt, and when they get drunk enough they even believe they can win back California. That kind of thinking equals a lot of dead greasers, eh, señora?"

"You are a devil!"

"Maybe, but I ain't one to make idle threats. You've heard what I've done so far. If this goes on much longer, I can't say what I might be responsible for doin'."

Michael didn't know if Love was bluffing or not, but he believed that the man was desperate enough to carry out his threat.

"All right," Michael said, "we'll help you."

"Good!" Love grunted, climbing back on his horse. "Now where is Murieta?"

"I'll need to join you," Michael said. "Since he moves around, I can't say where he might be at any one moment, but I can get you close enough so that you'll come across him and his men very soon."

Love didn't like the idea of taking Michael along, but it made sense. "Fair enough. Get your horse."

"Mind if I clean up, eat and join you in the morning?" Michael took his wife's hand. "A man needs time to say good-bye to his bride."

"Yeah, I heard about that," Love said. "Otherwise, I'd have been over here weeks ago paying her a visit."

"Stay the hell away from her," Michael warned.

Love squinted down at Michael and then growled before riding away: "Daybreak, Callahan. We'll be waiting for you about three miles west of town. Don't keep us waiting. I might just enjoy coming over and getting you out of bed."

"Go to hell!"

Love began to laugh as he rode away.

Seventeen

July 25, 1853

It is just after midnight and in a few hours we will be back
in the saddle. For the past few days, we have been camped
near a canyon known as Arroyo Cantua at the eastern edge of
the Coastal Range. The canyon has very steep sides and is
apparently a popular place for the Mexicans to hide stolen
horses. Four days ago we found about seventy Mexican
vaqueros and fifteen or twenty women holding a large horse
remuda estimated by the Rangers to number more than seven
hundred. The Mexicans claimed they were captured wild
mustangs.

Captain Love inspected each horse for a brand but only
seven or eight were found, and all of them Spanish. Even so,
Captain Love took several horses which he claimed to have
recognized as being stolen while the rest of us kept our hands
close to our guns. I thought sure that there would be a fight
because the vaqueros were very angry. But they did not fight,
probably because of their women. I think it was the presence
of the women which saved us because we could not have
defeated so many tough hombres.

Now, we are preparing to move up the canyon in the hope
of finding Joaquín Murieta. The Rangers are very tense. They
keep asking me again and again if I am sure that none of the

seventy vaqueros we saw was Joaquín Murieta. I tell them no but I am not sure that they believe me. They are ready to kill anyone in order to end this hardship and to claim their bounties.

I pray this will be over soon.

"WHAT THE HELL you keep writing in that damned diary for?" Love demanded.

Michael looked up at the captain. He knew that Harry Love was itching to explode in a killing rage.

"I like to put my thoughts down on paper."

"What for?"

"For posterity."

"Huh?"

"Never mind," Michael said, slipping the diary into his shirt pocket.

Love glared down at him. "We're gonna find that greaser come daybreak. I just got a feeling deep in my bones. That party of vaqueros had to have a leader and I'll bet anything that it was Joaquín and he was off close somewheres. But he'll come back. He won't leave that many stolen horses. My guess is that they're taking them on down to Los Angeles."

Michael stood up and met Love eye to eye. "Just don't get itchy with your trigger finger, Captain. I'm the only one that can positively identify Murieta and Three-fingered Jack."

"Ranger Byrnes says he thinks he can identify Murieta."

Michael scoffed at this news. "We both know he's never seen the real Joaquín Murieta in his life. And I won't falsify a report so that you can claim a reward for killing innocent men."

"Don't tell me that you think them greasers caught all those horses runnin' free."

"I don't know. You said yourself that all but a few were un-branded."

Love stared hard at Michael, and the corners of his mouth twisted downward with contempt. "Callahan, you're a damned

Mex lover and I got no use for a white man who likes Mexicans better than his own kind. You'd just better help us find Joaquín Murieta muy pronto."

Michael bit back an angry reply and Love stalked away. In the moonlight Michael could see the restless silhouettes of both men and horses, all tense and on edge. Farther out he noted the dark shapes of large oaks marching across rolling hills covered by withered grass.

None of the other Rangers would speak to him. To have shown him any friendliness would have been to take sides against Captain Love. No one dared do that. Michael thought about Aurora, Joaquín and himself. If he had the last few years to live all over again, he supposed that he would change very little except to somehow prevent that terrible night when Rosita had been killed and Joaquín flogged almost to death. That had been the turning point. After that night nothing except his marriage to Aurora had gone quite right. And now it seemed as if everything came down to what would happen in the next few hours.

Was Joaquín's plan going to work? If Joaquín Valenzuela and Three-fingered Jack and the most vicious of Joaquín Murieta's band were just up the canyon, as they were supposed to be, then within a few hours this story would end as planned. But if not, innocent vaqueros were going to die for no reason.

Time passed. Michael realized he had dozed when he was waked by a Ranger who grunted, "Get your horse saddled. We ride out in fifteen minutes."

Michael was on his feet and moving. He was mounted when Love raised his hand and signaled his men forward. A blood-red and angry sun was lifting to the east. Michael knew it was going to be another blistering day.

Ten minutes later a Ranger hissed, "Look up yonder, Captain!"

They had to squint to see the thin, wavery plume of smoke lifting up toward the sky.

"Spread out," Love ordered. "We'll come over that last hill on whoever the hell we find."

The Rangers spread out and Michael found himself the last man on the right flank. Love and Ranger Billy Henderson rode in the middle and slightly in the front. Michael could almost hear his heart banging against his rib cage. His racing heart, the creaking protest of saddle leather and the soft clip-clop of their horse's hooves on the hard, dry earth were the only sounds.

When they came over the last hill and gazed down, they saw eight Mexicans. Michael immediately recognized the thick form of Three-fingered Jack García.

"Boys," Love said as he kicked his horse into a trot and pulled his gun, "keep your guns ready and let me do the talking. Callahan, do you see Joaquín among them?"

"Not from this distance."

Love swore softly. "You better holler if you do, and make it loud and clear."

All of them glanced in Michael's direction, but his eyes were locked on Three-fingered Jack, who crouched by the fire roasting meat. So far the Mexicans had not seen them. Several were rolled up in their serapes and asleep. Michael could feel a flood of thick dread churning in his empty gut.

They stampeded down the hill and were about two hundred yards from the little camp when Three-fingered Jack and a handsome young Mexican who was bathing his horse in the canyon's stream glanced up. Three-fingered Jack shouted a warning. The sleeping Mexicans were instantly on their feet, grabbing their weapons.

Captain Love did not fire his gun but raced down the hill, followed by the other Rangers, and he yelled over and over, "Alto! Quién vive? Halt! Who's there?"

The Rangers encircled the eight Mexicans. Michael watched Three-fingered Jack very closely. The big, ugly killer was as tense as a coiled spring. He wasn't going to go down without a fight. But which one of these eight was Joaquín Valenzuela, the outlaw reported to be just as bloodthirsty as Garcia and who so enjoyed slitting the throats of defenseless Chinamen?

"What are you men doing here?" Love demanded in his own good Spanish. "Who are you?"

Three-fingered Jack growled something, and when he moved, Captain Love saw the missing index finger. "Ranger Chase, shoot that one if he moves again! Callahan, which one is Joaquín?" Love was screaming.

Michael did not know, and when he hesitated for a moment Ranger Byrnes shouted, "Captain, I think that's him! That's Joaquín!"

The Mexican in the stream who had been washing his sweat-crusted horse was unarmed. His eyes widened in alarm and at just that moment Three-fingered Jack García reached under his serape, drew a gun and fired twice at Captain Love. The first shot clipped off a lock of the Captain's long, greasy hair, but the second bullet went wild as the Rangers opened fire on all the Mexicans.

Three-fingered Jack slammed down across the campfire. Screaming and batting at fire and bullet holes, he rolled, jerked and twisted. Michael froze with his gun in his fist as the Mexicans attempted to return fire but were riddled on their feet.

"Joaquín is getting away!" someone cried.

Through the gunsmoke, Michael saw the vaquero he was now certain to be Joaquín Valenzuela leap onto his horse and send it racing upstream.

"Get him!"

Ranger Henderson was carrying a shotgun. He slammed it to his shoulder and fired, but his horse shied and he missed. Hurling the shotgun aside, Henderson sent his horse racing after the escaping Mexican. Love was shouting for everyone to go after Joaquín because every other Mexican was either dead or mortally wounded.

Michael spurred furiously after Henderson. He saw the Ranger fire twice more, and Joaquín's horse staggered, then fell.

Joaquín lit on his feet running. Henderson's horse closed the gap with a rush, and Michael saw twin puffs of gunsmoke erupt from the Ranger's pistol. Joaquín stumbled and reached toward his back, fingers splayed and already covered with blood.

Michael saw Joaquín come to a halt, sway on his feet and then turn to face the Ranger. Raising a hand, Joaquín cried, "Don't shoot me anymore. I'm dead!"

Ranger Henderson fired again, but his gun was empty. As Michael watched, several other Rangers overtook Henderson and, with the killing fever upon them, shot Joaquín full of holes.

"That *is* him!" Ranger Byrnes cried. "We finally got Joaquín Murieta and Three-fingered Jack!"

Love whirled his dancing horse around to face Michael. "He's right, isn't he!" It wasn't a question, it was a command.

"Yes," Michael heard himself say in a voice that was not his own.

"You hear that, boys, the goddamn Gringo Amigo here says that's his Murieta!"

Now that the legend who had stirred pride in every Mexican's heart was finally dead, the Rangers all dismounted and stood in a ring around Joaquín's body. Excited, they all talked at once. Someone grabbed Joaquín by the arm and rolled him over on his back, then said with contempt, "He sure don't look like much to me."

"He's worth a sight more than you would be dead," Ranger White said, causing the others to laugh too loud.

Michael had seen enough. He turned and rode back to the Mexican camp, still haunted by a veil of gunsmoke. Michael knew for a fact that these were the worst of Joaquín's band, the hand-chosen few that Murieta had been willing to set up for ambush. Every single man among them was a brutal, un- repentant killer, but the only real comfort Michael could salvage out of this bloody showdown was that the legend of Joaquín Murieta was dead as well.

A tortilla was burning in a heavy black frying pan, and even though Michael had not eaten since the previous evening, he had no appetite. He studied the dead banditos, wondering if there was some single incident or moment where, like the real

Joaquín Murieta, a gentle spirit had turned hard. These dark reflections ended when the Rangers returned with the corpse of Joaquín draped over the back of one of their horses. The Mexican's body was dumped unceremoniously beside that of Three-fingered Jack.

"Well, boys," Love said, looking at all of his men, "I guess we'll need evidence to prove we really did kill Joaquín Murieta and Three-fingered Jack. Don't want somebody sayin' we made this whole thing up just to collect the State's reward."

Michael saw one of the Rangers draw his huge bowie knife and step down from his horse. "I'll claim that honor, Captain."

"Go right ahead."

Michael's stomach flopped. He started to protest, but he knew that it would do no good and might even get him killed. He reined away from the Rangers so he didn't have to watch.

"Put Joaquín's head in that flour sack," Love commanded. "Hell, put Three-fingered Jack's head in there too, along with his right hand. There's no mistaking that one."

Michael took a deep, steadying breath and gripped his saddle horn. "I'm going home," he said, loud enough to be heard by every last damn one of them.

"You'll by God stay with us!" Love commanded. "I want you around in case anybody challenges me that this head really belonged to Joaquín."

Michael twisted around in his saddle. "You can go straight to hell, Captain Love!"

The big Texan paled and his hand moved toward his gun, but Michael was betting it was empty. And by the time the captain could reload, Michael was going to be a mile away, racing to the arms of his beautiful Spanish woman.

He spurred his horse into a run. If there was even one single unspent bullet among those twenty California Rangers, Michael figured it would end up in his back and he'd go down the same way as Joaquín Valenzuela.

But there were no shots, and he never looked back once all the way to Hornitos.

.   .   .   .

ONE WEEK LATER, Michael was driving a buckboard just east of San Diego. Beside him sat Aurora and behind them, covered with a tarp, Joaquín lay hidden and in more than a little pain as they rolled south toward Old Mexico. Joaquín had appeared in the night two days after Michael had returned to Hornitos. He'd fallen from his horse, his leg now badly infected and swollen twice its normal size.

They could not dare trust a gringo doctor. So Michael found an old woman who made steaming poultices of yerba del pasmo and forced Joaquín to drink the bitter purple herb tea she called "te de alsio," which was known to kill blood poisons.

While the entire Gold Country was feting Captain Love and his Rangers for at last putting an end to California's most famous bandito, Michael had driven the buckboard southward, always careful to avoid the towns and settlements. The moment travelers appeared, he was quick to warn the injured vaquero to pull the tarp over himself and his sacks of gold.

But on this hot afternoon with blistering winds lifting off the great Mojave Desert, Joaquín's fever had risen again. Because it was hot under the tarp, he lay panting in the wagon. "We have to find shade and stop," Aurora said anxiously. "And we're going to have to find a doctor."

Michael did not argue. He knew that Joaquín was in bad shape. Two miles farther, they came upon a stream with grass for the horses and plenty of shade trees. "I'll unhitch the team and ride one of the horses into San Diego."

Aurora nodded with a worried expression. "I am out of medicines."

"He'll live."

"But will he ever walk again?" Aurora whispered. "He is a vaquero first, last and always. What can a vaquero do if he cannot ride?"

"I'll ride," Joaquín gasped. "But right now I need whiskey."

"It would not be good for the fever!"

"Just a swallow. The leg is very painful, señora."

"Give him some whiskey," Michael said, glancing over his shoulder. "There are some trees just ahead. I'm going to find a doctor."

"No!" Joaquín lowered his voice. "I will be better when the day cools. You will see. Then we can go on. How much farther to the border?"

"Ten, twelve miles," Michael grunted as he climbed out of the buckboard and then helped Aurora down.

"Bueno!" Joaquín forced a wide smile. "At daybreak we will see the sunrise over Mexico. We will travel to Alamos, the land of my forefathers, and will buy a great rancho and live well forever."

"Just living seems enough, considering what's already happened," Aurora said.

" 'Just living,' señora, is never enough."

Aurora studied Joaquín, knowing he was right. She looked south toward Mexico. The prospect of a new life—new adventures, customs and friends—was one she welcomed. "We will grow old and happy together," she said, more to herself than to either of her companions.

IT WAS JUST BEFORE SUNDOWN when the three riders approached their camp.

"Got any supper you can spare?" one of them asked.

"I'm afraid we're about out of food ourselves," Michael said, watching their eyes measure him, Aurora and their horses.

The biggest one pretended not to hear as he dismounted. He was young, maybe Michael's own age, and he had a belligerent jaw, cold, deep-set eyes and a gun that rested much too comfortably on his hip.

"Then how about some coffee for me and my friends? I can see you've got a pot of it boiling."

Michael knew that he could not afford to let this kind of treacherous men join his camp. The only thing to do was take a hard stand and try to get rid of them in a hurry.

"I'm afraid you're mistaken. What's boiling is canutilla. That's Spanish for squaw tea."

The rider shrugged his broad shoulders. "Well, is that a fact! We never had any. Who knows, could be we'd like the stuff. Eh, boys?"

The other two nodded without enthusiasm.

"I don't think you'd like the taste of it," Aurora said, watching as one of the men rode over toward the buckboard, which was shaded by the tree and where Joaquín lay dozing.

"I'll bet I'd like a taste of *you,* though," the man said, with a wink of his eye.

"Now just a damn minute, mister," Michael said, reaching for his gun.

"Don't even think about it," the man warned, his own gun up and pointed at Michael's belly before he could clear leather.

Michael froze, knowing he would rather die than let another man touch Aurora.

"Michael, no!" Aurora cried, reading his thoughts.

"Hey, Troy!" the curious rider said, "There's a Mexican lyin' in here. A couple of saddles and . . . What the hell you got in them sacks, Greaser?"

The rider jumped down from his horse, grabbed a bag of gold, tore it open and cried, "Why it's—"

Whatever the rider was about to say was left unfinished as Joaquín's gun boomed and the man died, spilling gold dust. Beside Michael, Troy spun, and a bullet from his six-gun splintered the side of the buckboard. Michael drew his own gun and fired at almost point-blank range. Troy stiffened, tried to turn around. Michael shot him again.

Aurora screamed a warning. Michael looked up and saw the third rider point his gun at him and fire. A searing pain struck Michael in the ribs, and he felt himself crashing over backward, hitting the ground and rolling down into the stream.

He heard more gunfire, and then Aurora and Joaquín were at his side, pulling him out of the water, saying words that he struggled to understand.

"Amigo!" Joaquín choked.

Aurora was tearing off his shirt and sobbing hysterically.

Michael wanted to comfort her. "It doesn't feel bad at all, querida."

She began to speak Spanish so rapidly he could not have understood her even if his head was clear, which it was most definitely not.

"Am I going to die?"

"No!" she cried, ripping her skirt into strips and working frantically to stop the bleeding.

"The bullet passed through the body," Joaquín said.

"I'm not scared," Michael told them. "I fear death only half as much as being alone and unloved."

"You will *never* be alone," Aurora said, her tears washing his face.

"I must find a doctor!" Joaquín said, passing a hand weakly across his eyes.

But Michael gripped his friend's arm. "No. It is too risky and . . . there is no point, eh, señor? A doctor cannot change anything now. It is in God's own hands."

"But what can I do?"

"You can get us safely to Mexico," Michael told him. "I must see the plaza where the boys and girls circle and carry flowers each spring."

"You *will* see them!" Joaquín promised. "I swear it."

Michael closed his eyes because a great weariness was upon him. "Tell me that story, Joaquín. Leave out nothing."

"But, Amigo!"

"All right," Michael said quietly, "leave out the small details. But tell it and then put me in the wagon. Aurora will drive the team and we will ride side by side. And when the night is almost gone, we will stop and have a little whiskey and watch the sunrise over Mexico."

"Sí!"

Joaquín took Michael's hand, and the vaquero slipped back in time, to his childhood when he was a simple boy with simple dreams, clutching a wildflower.

"In the spring," Joaquín began, "when the wildflowers bloom and the hills are yellow, red and gold, the children of Alamos become very excited. And on the special feast day of . . ."

Michael's mind floated away. He could smell the flowers, hear the laughter of children, see the soft, warm hills ablaze with color. He smiled. It would be good to live in Mexico. Did the old chapel there have a fine church bell? If not, perhaps a little of the gold could be spent to buy one. It's toll would ring out in a joyous chorus with the children's singing and laughter.

He would have to speak to Joaquín about the church bell. But that could wait at least until sunrise, after he had slept.

Author's Note

THE LEGEND of Joaquín Murieta continues to fascinate, confound and serve as an endless source of historical debate. The "Ghost of Sonora" remains the quintessential mythical horseman, the great El Patricio of the West who returned ethnic pride to an oppressed Mexican people suffering great injustices after losing California in the Bear Flag Revolution.

I don't believe that any serious historians doubt that there were many superb Mexican vaqueros in California during the Forty-Niner Gold Rush who turned against the law. The newspaper accounts, accurately referenced and quoted throughout this novel, make it very clear that a Mexican named Joaquín did, for a few bloody and exciting months early in 1853, exert terror among the inhabitants of the southern gold fields. What does remain in doubt is if this bandito's name was, in fact, Joaquín Murieta. And if it was, did he become a famous outlaw because of an outrage against his wife and a flogging that left him near death? What cannot be argued is that a small band of Mexicans, including outlaws thought to be Joaquín Murieta and the vicious Three-fingered Jack García, were killed by Captain Harry Love and his Rangers on July 25, 1853.

For years afterward, Joaquín's head had quite a story of its own. Exhibited all over California by Harry Love and several others, the head attracted large crowds willing to pay the munificent sum of one dollar in order to gape and stare with morbid fascination at the grisly trophies. When the crowds finally began to dwindle, the San Francisco *Alta,* on February 10, 1856, reported that "The head and hand [actually Three-fingered Jack's hand] of the celebrated guerrilla robber, Joaquín, have been purchased by Mr. Craigmiles of this city, who leaves on the next steamer with his ghastly property, for New Orleans. He intends exhibiting them through the interior cities of the United States, and wintering them at New York. He confidently expects to realize $50,000 with his speculation."

By 1881 the head and hand were permanent attractions in San Francisco at the Pacific Museum, where this novel begins with Senator Paddy Ryan just a few days after the devastation in 1906. It took that great act of nature to allow the supposed head of Joaquín to achieve its well-deserved and final rest, probably somewhere under the rebuilt city.

Over the next century, more and more evidence has been found to support the thesis that the head displayed so many years did not belong to the real Joaquín Murieta, who probably escaped to Mexico and lived to a very ripe old age. It is said that Joaquín's bones lie in the old Jesuit cemetery of Cucupe, high in the Sierra Madre Mountains of Sonora.

And though this story is fiction, Joaquín might well have needed help to plot a ruse that would allow him to escape California without being forever hounded by the law. If so, I would like to think that friends or lovers like Michael Callahan, the Gringo Amigo, and the beautiful Aurora are resting in that Jesuit cemetery too.

ABOUT THE AUTHOR

GARY MCCARTHY is the author of the Darby Buckingham novels published in the Double D Western line, along with many other Western and historical novels. His most recent Double D Western is *Blood Brothers*. He lives in Ojai, California.